SHOOT TO LIVE

Sheriff Jim Strange had been falsely accused and two hired guns were in the shadows waiting to kill him. But Jim had no intention of dying! Nevertheless, all the odds were stacked against him and his one hope lay with the oddly assorted passengers he was to hide amongst on the ill-fated stage bound for Fort Benham. There were many questions to be answered. Why, for example, was the trail littered with so many bodies, and would Jim be the next victim?

DAN CLAYMAKER

SHOOT TO LIVE

Complete and Unabridged

LINFORD
Leicester

First published in Great Britain in 2000 by
Robert Hale Limited
London

First Linford Edition
published 2001
by arrangement with
Robert Hale Limited
London

British Library CIP Data

Claymaker, Dan
  Shoot to live.—Large print ed.—
  Linford western library
  1. Western stories
  2. Large type books   WES
  I. Title   127/649
  823.9′14 [F]

  ISBN 0–7089–9749–X

Published by
F. A. Thorpe (Publishing)
Anstey, Leicestershire

Set by Words & Graphics Ltd.
Anstey, Leicestershire
Printed and bound in Great Britain by
T. J. International Ltd., Padstow, Cornwall

This book is printed on acid-free paper

This for F.H.
who would play her part perfectly!

1

They would be waiting, back of the Sweetcall Bar, just as they always were when there was business to be done and the deal was a killing.

Two of them: Joe Reisner, one-time fast gun with the Bonaldi outfit out Kansas way; wanted on a dozen counts of armed robbery, murder, rape and pillage; mean-eyed and twitchy in his gathering years, but still one of the fastest on the draw to a holstered Colt.

Pete Lenski, ten years Reisner's junior, with a reputation for gunslinging since his troubled teens; always two steps ahead of the law and just one behind any man fool enough to cross him; known principally for his addiction to quality whiskey and fancy women; a gun for hire whenever the price was right.

The pair had joined up two years

1

back, dodging Marshal Sam Pettifer's posse hunting down the perpetrators of the November bank heist at Norville, and been plying their killing trade ever since. Name the target, clinch the deal and Reisner and Lenski would spread the lead.

All in a day's work; just a way of life.

But on this day, in the dusty heat of the high afternoon in the Midwest town of Reuben, there was a hitch to their well-laid plans. Their intended victim was late, and that, if nothing else, was worrying.

Reisner had growled his disapproval of the timing at the outset. 'Ain't one for day killin' and well yuh know it,' he had told Lenski who had brought the deal to the table two days earlier following a meeting with local land-owner, Moran Beattie. 'And that don't take no count of who's payin'. And 'sides,' he had added behind a rumbling belch, 'we ain't never come to shootin' out-of-luck lawmen.'

That much at least was true. Name

your target, sure enough, but keep it clear of notoriety, had been their simple byword since forming the partnership. Big names with a big past were trouble; too many shadows catching up; too many grievances unfulfilled. And there were plenty lurking in the steps of the former Sheriff of Franckton.

Jim Strange had set high standards for his town and the folk living in it. Cross the law, bend it, abuse it, and you paid the price. No quarter, no dealing, and none, among the generally peace-loving inhabitants of Franckton, expected. But visitors, especially gun-happy roustabouts with money to burn and an appetite for all the fire they could spark, were not so familiar with Sheriff Strange's ways.

And that had applied particularly to the Beattie boys on the day they hit Franckton homeward bound for Reuben after their spring drive to the railhead at Denver.

They had sure as hell been in some mood for shaking off the trail dirt on that day. Booze, girls, gambling and still more booze had been the only priorities, and Franckton, in its canny wisdom for making the most of loose pockets while the going was good, had responded.

A mite too generously in Jim Strange's view when the drink eventually took its hold, the girls' allure begun to pall and wild, whiskey-hazed eyes looked for alternative entertainments.

Fire broke out in the bar, fists flew for no good reason anybody ever remembered, and in the general mêlée and mayhem shots were fired — any amount of them, frenzied and foolishly and finally, close on midnight, fatally, killing Moran Beattie's younger son, Arran, where he stood stripped down to his underwear in the middle of the street.

Cattle king and land baron, Beattie, backed by his wealth, his influential power among the elected political brokers back East, and not least the threat of his 'distraught' hired hands

4

— had lost no time in laying the blame for Arran's shooting squarely at the door of Sheriff Strange.

'Fella ain't fit to herd steers, let alone strut the street behind the badge of the law,' he had pronounced far and wide through a dozen counties, neighbouring states and into just about any ear that would listen or found itself dragged close enough to suffer the spit of his venom.

Upshot had been the ignominious stripping three months later of the badge from Strange, his banishment from the town and 'places thereabouts' and his departure, some reckoned, for the wild lands west of anywhere beyond the Big Cut river bend. They had seen the last of Jim Strange.

Until, that is, he had turned up, weathered, worn, but sharp-eyed and watchful as ever right there in Reuben . . .

'What's he fool enough to be here for, anyhow?' Joe Reisner had muttered in his growing reluctance. 'Damnit, got the whole country to go at, so what's the thinkin' in good as steppin' up to Beattie's front door? He askin' to get himself killed or somethin'?'

'Mebbe he's figurin' on pleadin' his innocence,' Lenski had sneered. 'But t'ain't for us to fathom, is it? Who cares? There's ten thousand in crisp bills on offer for takin' him out, no mess, no questions. Ten thousand . . . Now we ain't for turnin' our backs on that sorta payout, are we? Not us, not the way we do things. Easy as puttin' lead in a barn door. So you just reckon it, my friend. A whole ten thousand . . . enough to take us clear of this dirt-baked town to anywheres we have a mind for. What yuh say to Mexico? What about that? All them *hacienda* days and *señoritas* sittin' at yuh feet? Yuh fancy that for a simple shootin'?'

The fact was that Joe Reisner fancied just such a prospect. And why not? No hiding the years, was there? No disputing that restful days to peaceful nights when a fellow could sleep easy were a whole sight more appealing than rousting it with the young bloods the likes of Lenski. *Haciendas, señoritas* and the money to keep them in a manner befitting his needs was a future he could handle.

One last shooting, taking out a dirt-weary, down-on-his-luck lawman, no mess, no questions ... for ten thousand and a fast trail south? Why not?

★ ★ ★

'Four days he's been in town; four days he's been steppin' into this bar, same time for the same drink. So where's he today? Why ain't he here? Answer me that.'

Lenski drummed an impatient finger on the table in the shadowed corner of the Sweetcall Bar, licked his lips and tightened his gaze on the batwings and the bustling, sunlit street beyond them. 'Know your trouble, Joe?' he

7

murmured, without turning his gaze on his partner. 'Age is gettin' yuh to frettin' somethin' chronic. Where's all that patient waitin' yuh were always boastin' on? Time was when yuh'd sit out a whole night for a shootin'.'

'Sure I would,' growled Reisner, 'and that's the point, ain't it? That was sittin' out a whole *night* — not this, middle of the afternoon, with darn near everybody in town waitin' on the stage loadin' up. Said from the start — '

'Yeah, yeah, I know what yuh said. Said it more times than I had m'self whores. Yuh beginnin' to sound like some rockin' chair old-timer!'

'And that's somethin' you can bet to,' growled Reisner again. 'I get m'self to Mexico and one of them sweetsmellin' *haciendas*, and a rockin' chair is just precisely what I'll be stickin' right there in the shade. You see if I don't. Tell yuh somethin' else — '

'Save it, Joe, I fancy we got company.'

There was never any mistaking the presence of Jim Strange in a town's

8

main street, bustling or otherwise. That had been his mark back in Franckton. Tall, soft-walking, same easy pace, arms loose and relaxed, fingers fully stretched as if waiting on a command; broad-brimmed hat always set tight and low so that you never truly saw his eyes until the gleam of them settled on you.

No push, no rush about Jim Strange. Every inch the presence of the law, with or without the badge.

'He armed?' said Reisner, squinting through the smoke-hazed gloom to the batwings.

'Single piece. Colt. Holstered high. Right side.'

'How high?'

'Too high. He ain't for spoilin'.'

'I heard say as how he always wears his Colt high.'

'Yuh been listenin' to rumour, Joe.'

Reisner grunted and flattened his hands on the table. 'Where's he now?' he hissed, sucking on the gaps in his teeth.

'Yuh mean to say yuh can't see him?'

9

frowned Lenski, his gaze ahead still tight.

''Course I can. Just wanted to make sure you could!'

It was just 2.30 by the clock in the Sweetcall Bar when Jim Strange stepped to the boardwalk fronting the batwings and spread a long-fingered left hand to push them open.

2

They would debate for years the hell that erupted in those next few minutes in the Sweetcall Bar on that hot afternoon in the Midwest town of Reuben.

Some reckoned as how Jim Strange's Colt was drawn and blazing lead before the batwings had parted; some that Pete Lenski had fired first and missed; others that Joe Reisner never set a hand to butt in the raging roar of shooting that splintered timber, shattered glass, scattered folk and brought the bustling street to a shuddering halt.

What is for sure, and was there for all to see, was the sight of Strange standing tall and silent and staring at the slumped, blood-soaked body of Reisner and finally giving the scurrying shape of Lenski, heading fast as his legs would carry him for the livery, no more than a casual, uninterested glance.

But there was a whole riot of activity soon as the gunsmoke had cleared. Strange holstered his piece, and Jonas Lyman, town undertaker, cleared his throat politely and ran the tip of his pencil through a gulp of bitter-tasting spittle.

A bar girl groaned and fainted; another screamed and sobbed uncontrollably. A pot man crunched through shards of broken glass. Winning hands of cards lay where they had spilled from trembling fingers. Four men fought in a scramble of limbs to be first through the back door; some came slowly to their feet from drink-swilling tables, some made to head for the 'wings, but thought better of it at the sight of Strange, unmoved and still staring.

Then somebody yelled for somebody to 'go get the sheriff' and pushed over a chair in his anxiety to be the one to do it. Others took up the call and began to swarm as if to pour like bees to the already crowded boardwalk where onlookers craned and jostled for a view of the body.

It was Sheriff Frank O'Grady's bellowing roar of 'Stand clear there, the lot of yuh!' that settled the threatened mob reaction, parted the throng and gave him passage to stride, Winchester firm in his grip, through the 'wings and into the gloomy, smoke-filled bar.

Nobody lays claim to hearing precisely what it was O'Grady murmured into Strange's ear, only that in the few seconds it took for him to say it Strange neither shifted so much as a finger nor blinked an eye. And when O'Grady was done, there was no more than an almost gentle handing over to him of the man's gunbelt and Colt, a quiet stare between the two of them and a slow, unhurried turn to leave the bar. Not so much as a glance at the bleeding body — 'like it was never there,' as one old-timer put it.

Last anybody saw of Jim Strange on that day was him being marched ahead of a levelled Winchester to the town jail.

'Just what the hell do yuh think yuh doin'? Yuh got the slightest notion, so much as a drift of thought through that numbskull stubborn head of yours, that yuh standin' within a spit of bein' hanged, mebbe lynched, at best shot through 'til there ain't nothin' of yuh worth nailin' down a coffin for? Any of that occurred to you by any remote chance?'

Sheriff Frank O'Grady strode the length of his dusty, cluttered office, reached the smeared window, squinted through it, turned and strode back to the cell door, hands tight in a writhing grip behind his back.

'No, it ain't, has it?' he grunted. 'Yuh got yuh eyes set on just one thing and yuh ain't seein' nothin' else. Nothin' at all. Ain't that the way of it? Right, aren't I? And don't you dare stand there and say other!'

Jim Strange sighed, shifted his weight and opened his mouth to speak.

'I ain't listenin'!' snapped O'Grady. 'Damn it, I ain't got the time. I gotta think this through, get yuh outa this hole yuh dug for y'self. And don't think I'll be doin' it in a benevolent frame of mind, 'cos I shan't. Not no how.' He groaned, broke the grip and let his arms hang loose at his sides. 'Hell, Jim,' he croaked, 'how could yuh do this — and in my town? My town of all places, f'Cris'sake!'

'Yuh know the answer to that well as I do,' said Strange.

'Oh, sure — sure I do,' he quipped again. 'I let yuh into my town against my better judgement — should've had yuh ride on when I had the chance: fed yuh, watered yuh, had yuh sleepin' in that jail bed back of yuh, damnit. Even had the decency to warn yuh against them gunslingin' rats, Reisner and Lenski, and how it might just be that Beattie would recruit them to his payroll once news got to him yuh were in town. But, hell, I didn't figure for yuh stayin' on to face up to a

15

showdown with 'em. Why didn't yuh leave? Yuh had no cause to go pickin' a fight. Yuh could've ridden out any time, anywhere — '

'I done with the ridin', Frank. Ridden all I got a mind for. Time's come to put that Franckton business to rights. I no more shot Arran Beattie than walked on the moon. But I know who did.'

'Yeah, yeah,' said O'Grady, easing away from the desk, 'so yuh said, a dozen times. But I don't wanna hear it, Jim, not now I don't. I got only one consideration: how to get yuh outa this town, alive and in one piece, before Beattie gets to hear of the shootin' here, 'cos when he does . . . ' He rubbed his chin as he moved back to the window. 'Well, mebbe there is a way,' he mused softly. 'Assumin' I got the time to get organized.'

O'Grady swung round to stare at the clock on the wall behind him. 'An hour,' he murmured, settling his hat.

'Ain't no call for you to get involved

deeper than yuh are,' said Strange, gripping the bars of the cell door. 'I done what I done 'cos I had no choice. Soon as yuh told me them gunslingin' scum were in town, didn't take no fathomin' to figure I'd be carryin' a price worth killin' for. Had no plans for them to collect. So, get me my horse back of here and I'll be gone faster than yuh can blink, and grateful to yuh for the chance. All I'm askin', Frank.'

'You just ride outa here and yuh'll have Beattie and his boys on yuh tail faster than a rattler's bite. Hell, he's got men enough to scour this territory for a hundred miles in any direction. And don't f'get — there's Lenski on the loose. I wouldn't give a drunk's bad breath for him not still reckonin' on claimin' the price on yuh head.' O'Grady crossed to the window again. 'Only fair chance yuh got of grabbin' some time on your side is for it to *look* as if yuh pulled a fast one over me, got clear and set yuh sights on the border — 'ceptin', o'course, yuh won't be doin' nothin' of the kind.'

'And just how — ' began Strange, his knuckles whitening on the bars.

'Just leave the thinkin' and doin' to me, will yuh?' grunted O'Grady, wiping a hand over a smeared window-pane. 'And don't even get to askin' me why I'm doin'this. Mebbe I'm lookin' to my own skin — not that Beattie'll see it that way — or mebbe I'm just a mite grateful yuh got Reisner and Lenski outa my hair at long last.'

He turned and walked slowly back to his desk, collected the cell keys from a drawer, slammed it shut and stared long and hard into Strange's eyes. 'I get yuh outa this town, yuh stay out, yuh hear? Just go settle yuh differences some place else!'

'Want me to tell yuh why yuh doin' this?' said Strange, his lips flickering over a soft grin. 'Yuh just happen to believe I didn't shoot the Beattie boy, don't yuh?'

'Yeah, well, that's as mebbe,' shrugged O'Grady, jangling the bunch of keys. 'Let's just give yuh the chance to prove it, shall we? If we get lucky . . . '

3

'It's a privilege, ma'am, a real privilege. Why, I wouldn't have figured in my wildest dreams for somethin' like this happenin' to somebody like me. Not no way, I wouldn't.' The round-faced, podgy-fingered man perched in the corner-seat of the swaying stage adjusted his metal-framed spectacles into the bridge of his nose, tweaked the folds of the silk cravat at his neck and brushed a loose, nervous hand over the roll of his frock coat lapels. 'Hiram J. Pepperthwaite at your service, ma'am,' he smiled sumptuously.

The woman seated opposite returned the smile with the faintest flicker of her carefully puckered lips, flashed the man an acknowledging glance, ran a careful hand over the shapely thigh beneath the drift of her satin dress, and leaned back. 'How kind,' she murmured, flicking open the fan in her lap.

' 'Course, we ain't never met,' smiled Pepperthwaite again. 'I mean, not face on, we ain't. But I seen yuh, ma'am, sure have, must be close on a dozen times now. First caught yuh at the Palace in Denver. Hell — beggin' yuh pardon — that was some performance yuh gave back there. Lady Macbeth like I ain't never seen before.' He nodded quickly to his fellow passengers. 'That's Shakespeare, 'case yuh ain't familiar.'

The sleeping man merely grunted and sank his face deeper behind the depths of his tipped hat. The large, lace-ruffled, corseted lady in a hat alive with feathers huffed and turned a disdainful gaze to the swirling dust of the sun-blazed land, her gloved hand seeking a steadying grip as the stage bounced and creaked to the spread of the trail.

'And then there was *Midsummer Night's Dream* at Mount Creasey,' continued Pepperthwaite, still smiling. 'Caught yuh again at Marshall Town, twice at Moore's Creek, the last night at Palmerson, and damnit if I didn't get to the front row time yuh opened at Jake's Bend. Some occasion that was! Why, do yuh know, ma'am, I was darned near — '

'Yuh been stalkin' the lady like some sick dog or somethin', mister?' grunted the sleeping man from behind the hat.

Pepperthwaite stiffened and pushed his spectacles higher. 'I would have you know, sir, that Miss Francine Devaux here is one of our finest — not to say most handsome, if I may be so bold — exponents of the thespian arts we have seen in many years, and I for one consider it a privilege — '

'So yuh said,' murmured the man. 'Heard yuh the first time. Well, mebbe Miss Devaux would like to get some rest 'tween here and the swing station at Cooney. That so, lady?'

'I really have no — ' began the woman.

'She would!' snapped the sleeping

man, swallowing on a groan. 'And so would I!'

Pepperthwaite fingered his cravat and leaned closer to Francine Devaux. 'Pay the fella no heed, ma'am,' he smiled softly, his eyes ranging like lights over the woman's face. 'Day'll dawn when he'll realize the privilege he's slept through and be all the sadder for it.' He nodded knowingly and leaned closer. 'Meantime, don't you fret none. I'm booked all the way through to Fort Benham, and I guess you are too. Doin' a show there for the garrison? Lucky fellas. God willin', I'll catch it before my business there is through. But tell me,' he went on, lowering his voice to a whisper, 'why yuh travellin' alone, ma'am? Would've reckoned for a lady of your standin' bein' accompanied wherever she went.'

'Force of circumstances,' said the woman quietly. 'A hastily arranged engagement. My companions will be following shortly.'

'I see, I see,' nodded Pepperthwaite.

'Then lucky for you I happened along, eh?' He rolled his eyes. 'Heck there, what am I sayin' — lucky for you? Lucky for me!' He leaned back, drew a large bandanna from his pocket, flourished it and mopped his brow. 'What a day . . . '

'That, sir, is a considerable understatement!' huffed the lace-ruffled lady, her double chins heaving menacingly. 'I take it you witnessed that outrage in the town we've thankfully just left? Nothing short of wild lawlessness, not to say blatant murder. My husband shall hear of it the minute we reach Fort Benham.' She spread her fingers through the jungle of feathers in her hat. 'I should never have stayed so long in Denver.'

'Your husband, ma'am?' enquired Pepperthwaite. 'He bein'?'

'Colonel Fitzsimmons, of course,' huffed the woman. 'Garrison Commander at Benham.'

'The very same man I am due to meet,' grinned Pepperthwaite. 'Supplies business, you understand.'

'Really,' said the woman haughtily.

'Gerald,' murmured Francine Devaux, with a poised flick of the fan.

'Gerald?' hissed Mrs Fitzsimmons. 'You know my husband, Miss Devaux?'

'Quite well — from some time back, naturally. My engagement at the fort is at his invitation.'

The double chins heaved again. 'Strange my husband has never mentioned you.'

'Well, now,' quipped Pepperthwaite, pocketing the bandanna, 'small world, ain't it just? Who'd have figured for it?'

The sleeping man in the corner seat sighed and tipped his hat to deepen the shadow. Francine Devaux smiled softly to herself behind the fan.

Hiram Pepperthwaite settled his podgy hands on his knees and blinked furiously. 'Seems like the only good thing to come outa that black-hearted town we just left is the companionship we've found. Best forget the rest, don't you agree? All behind us now, anyhow.'

The stage rolled on to the creak of timbers, rumble of wheels and crack of a whip in the jangle of tack.

★ ★ ★

Spruce Wethers was in no frame of mind for an easy ride. This was going to be the fastest Reuben to Fort Benham stage run in the ten-year history of the line.

Yessir, and no messing, he thought, the reins to the already fast-paced team stinging in the grip of his gnarled, calloused hands, his eyes narrowed to watery slits against the rush of the hot wind and flying dust. Another hour, maybe less if the team proved willing, to the overnight stay at the swing station at Cooney Forks, crack of dawn start for the run to High Point, there in the day and just one more on the short-cut trail through Grey Rocks and Two Knees Canyon to Benham.

Get this whole miserable run off his back, and Amen to that; worst in all the years he had been behind the reins, and no thanks to that Sheriff O'Grady back there in Reuben. Hell, decent fellow he might be, but he sure knew how to push the power of the badge pinned to his shirt. Good as spelled out his 'askin' for a favour' like a military order . . .

'Yuh seen what happened here,' he had snapped, pacing the airless confines of the back room at the stage office. 'Trouble, big as it comes, and I ain't for havin' it on my porch. Lenski's runnin' free, God knows where, but he ain't goin' to let the killin' of his partner pass without some lead flyin' somewhere. And I ain't lookin' forward one mite to Beattie's reaction once this hits him . . . So you, Spruce, are goin' to do me a real favour. You're goin' to get that stage rollin' for Cooney as soon as yuh can. Three miles short of it, at the Spencer Bend, yuh'll find a lone man, horseless, hot and tired. That'll be Jim Strange. Yuh'll pick him up, take him on to Cooney, let him spend the night there and wave him goodbye at sun-up.

Yuh got that, Spruce? No questions. Just do it . . . '

So he would. Did he have a choice?

Not a man any part of the territory who would not stand to Jim Strange over the raw deal that had driven him out of Franckton. And not a man standing in Reuben who would not buy him a whole bottle of the best for ridding the world of Joe Reisner.

Something else, though, when it came to having him 'on the run' aboard the Reuben-Fort Benham stage.

No saying, was there, how that motley bunch of passengers back of him might react? They had all been in town, all seen the shooting. Take that actress, Miss Devaux. Smart, good-looking, but no saying to her venom if she got spitting to a temper. And that pecky salesman, Pepperthwaite, was just the sort to go opening his mouth away ahead of his thinking. As for Mrs Fitzsimmons — hell, he could just hear the outrage once she reached Benham, if not long before! Quiet fellow with the sleepy eyes was not so easy to read. He might be anybody.

Carriageload of almighty unknowns when you came to it. Well, Jim Strange, pondered Spruce through another crack of the whip, you would just have to take it as you found it . . .

'I ain't happy goin' along of this,' shouted Fishbone riding shotgun at Spruce's side. 'We ain't never done nothin' like this before. Not that I ain't for Jim Strange, yuh understand.'

'First time for everythin',' answered Spruce, tightening his grip.

'Supposin' Lenski's on the loose hereabouts,' shouted Fishbone again, cradling his Winchester into a new position across his knees. 'Supposin' Beattie gets to figurin' O'Grady's back of Strange's disappearance. Damnit, trail from here to Benham could get knee-deep in lead.' He spat high into the wind and ducked instinctively. 'Tell yuh somethin' else, Walt Petcham at the station ain't goin' to be no smilin' welcome when we pull in with a wanted man needin' an overnight bed.'

'Yuh get too easy to frettin', Fish-bone,' called Spruce, craning against a swirl of dust. 'We pick up Strange, take him to Cooney, and he's on his own. Bought himself some time, ain't he? Deservin' of it too in my book. Damnit, least we can do. Where's the harm, f'Cris'sake?'

'Seated right back of yuh!' yelled Fishbone. 'Yuh know how payin' passengers can be when it comes to comforts.'

'You just keep yuh eyes skinned and leave the passengers to me.'

'Gladly!' Fishbone spat and ducked another stream of wind-whipped spittle. 'Spencer Bend comin' up, and there's our man, right on time.' He hugged the Winchester into his lap. 'Last call to prayers!'

Spruce Wethers cracked the reins defiantly.

4

To the passing drifter who might have been scanning the dusty trail from the hill range above Spencer Bend, it might have seemed a mite strange to see the fortnightly stage from Reuben to Fort Benham slither, creak and grind to a halt at the raised arm of the lone man hailing it on its express run to Cooney Forks.

Stage had never been known to stop for the casual bystander, whatever the cut of his appearance, and never under any circumstances, barring accident or blatant hold-up, with Spruce Wethers in the driving seat and the reins tight in his grip. Spruce was in charge once aboard, Fishbone settled along of him, the doors closed and the wheels rolling, and nothing short of disaster would disturb the rigorous timetable.

But on this day, with still more than

an hour to the first drift of dusk, things were different.

The stage halted, Spruce exchanged a few words with the waiting man, doors opened, faces peered inquisitively, the man climbed aboard, doors slammed shut and the stage rolled on. All over in a matter of minutes, no fuss, no quibbling, almost, the drifter might have thought, watching the stage disappear in a sun-dappled swirl of dust, as if it were everyday, a regular thing for a fellow with the right connections.

He would not have known, of course, of the particular circumstances surrounding Jim Strange's arrival aboard the stage for Benham, though he might have queried just who it was rode off, once the stage was out of sight, trailing a spare, full saddled mount on the trail back to Reuben. Might too have caught just a glimpse of the gleam in the late afternoon sun of what for all the world looked very like a sheriff's badge pinned to the rider's shirt.

But, being a drifter, he would have simply shrugged and drifted on.

* * *

The sun was a dying blaze against the backdrop of the sprawl of the eastern hill range when Spruce closed the Benham stage on the silhouetted shapes of the Cooney Forks swing station.

He had driven the team hard and fast, no slackening the pace and with only a passing thought to the comfort of his passengers. Cooney, in Spruce's reckoning, could not come up soon enough on this run: get there on time, the travelling folk settled for the night, the team looked to and, top priority, Jim Strange off his back and as far from his stage as a fast, fresh horse from Walt Petcham's corral would carry him.

'No hard feeling,' he would say when the one-time sheriff was mounted up and set to ride, 'but I gotta look to my responsibilities here. Four folk and a heap of baggage to deliver safe and in one piece at Benham. Wish yuh well, Jim, but yuh gotta see it my way . . . '

And he would; he was that sort of fellow. He would know the risk Spruce was taking, know that O'Grady had done his best by him — know too that with Lenski on the loose and Moran Beattie foiled in his attempt for bitter revenge there would be no holding the pair of them once they got to tempering their anger with straight thinking. Rattlers spooked from their nest would be nothing along of their venom. But Jim Strange would see it that way, sure enough; mount up, ride out, take his chance with a head start a whole sight better than might have seemed possible back there in Reuben. He would make out, no question. He was just that sort of fellow . . .

'Ain't a lick of smoke at the station,' called Fishbone above the creaking grind and roll of the stage, his eyes narrowed on the looming shapes. 'So what's with Walt? He given up cookin' or somethin'?'

'Too free with the bottle midday more like,' shouted Spruce, easing the team to a bend in the trail, his grip on the reins tightening against a sticky sweat.

'T'ain't like Walt,' called Fishbone again. 'He ain't usually one for liquor 'til after sundown.'

Spruce leaned to the swinging pace. 'Mebbe he's been celebratin'. Could be it's his birthday.'

'Birthday?' scowled Fishbone. 'Walt Petcham ain't had a birthday in twenty years. Wouldn't know it, anyhow. Once told me as how he was born and raised in a pack of prairie coyotes. Reckons as how he was near full grown before he set eyes on a white man. Know somethin' else? Walt was . . . ' He leaned forward, his hands spreading like brackish pools over the Winchester. 'What the hell!' he moaned, the gaze narrowing to tight slits. 'Yuh see that, Spruce? Yuh see that corral?'

He saw it clear enough, only too well in the glowing blaze of the sunset and the softer spread of light from the station lanterns; saw it like a sudden haunting, the chill with it in the ooze of cold sweat across his back.

The corral was empty, not a horse in sight, the barred entrance standing like a waiting space, the silence brooding in the stark, deep shadows.

'Just what in hell's name . . . ' moaned Fishbone again. 'Walt gone ravin' crazed?'

Spruce heaved on the reins, slowing the team, lifting the creaks of the stage, grind of the wheels, to an echoing scream as they eased to the new pace.

'Yuh don't reckon, do yuh, as how — ' began Fishbone.

'Just don't let nobody step down minute we pull in,' said Spruce, his hands working feverishly at the reins. 'Keep them folk calm and outa sight 'til we seen what's goin' on here.'

'I'll tell yuh what's goin' on! Don't need no — '

'Shut it, Fishbone! Leave this to me. And don't go mouthin' off, yuh hear?'

Spruce rolled the stage to a halt at the station veranda, fastened the reins and had jumped to the still hot dirt before the team had quivered to rest.

He hitched his pants, spat the dust from his lips and glanced quickly at the deserted corral. Nothing more to be discovered there, he reckoned, turning to the dimly lit station and the open door in the depths of the shadowed veranda. No sight, no sound of a presence. He gulped and moved carefully to the steps. Just where, in tarnation, was Walt? And just why was that ceaselessly yapping hound of his not raising so much as a whimper?

'Hell!' he croaked on a stinging swallow, too tensed and sweat-soaked now to hear the soft click of a handle under pressure and the creak of worn hinges as the stage doors swung free.

★　★　★

Nothing moved, not even a fly, on the tired, humid air. The shadows were

37

spread like sleeping beasts from the limp glow of the lantern light. Shapes among chairs, tables, a side dresser, the bulk of the stone-built fireplace, the clutter of cooking pots and pans, seemed to lurk as if waiting to pounce. And there might not have been a sound to disturb had Spruce Wethers swallowed on the groan that rumbled deep in his parched throat at the sight of Walt sprawled face-down, his dog lifeless and glassy-eyed at his side, in a fast congealing pool of blood.

'In the name of the Devil's hell . . . ' he croaked, blinked, shuddered and groaned again, his fingers twitching on stinging nerve-ends, eyes bulging then narrowing as his body stiffened to a chilled numbness.

'Just what precisely is — ' The booming voice of Mrs Fitzsimmons at Spruce's back slid to a stifled intake of breath as she flounced across the veranda to the room in a breeze of feathers and wafting lavender.

'Oh, my God!' squeaked Hiram Pepperthwaite, stumbling to her side, his spectacles slipping to the tips of his flared nostrils.

Francine Devaux gasped and hid her face behind the spread of her fan.

The sleeping man backed to the shadows without making a sound.

Jim Strange eased softly, silently to the body and stared at it.

'I thought I said for you folks not to — ' flustered Fishbone, pushing his way to Spruce's side on a shuffling squeak of worn boot leather.

No one moved or spoke then for seconds that seemed to drift to minutes. Mrs Fitzsimmons fingered the feathers in her hat as if trying to hide them. Pepperthwaite sweated and gazed open-mouthed. Francine Devaux's eyes stayed unblinking behind the rim of the fan. The sleeping man shifted his weight. Jim Strange placed his hands on his hips.

'Out! Back to the stage the lot of you,' grunted Spruce, spreading his arms as he turned to usher the women from the room.

'That's right, that's right — out!' echoed Fishbone, slinging his Winchester to a two-handed grip.

'Well, really, this is all too much,' blustered the colonel's wife in another waft of lavender and creak of her corsets. 'My husband shall hear of this, and when he does — '

'Sure, sure,' soothed Spruce, herding the woman to the veranda. 'Just do like I say, ma'am, 'til I get this sorted. Ain't no sight here for a lady's eyes. You too, Miss Devaux, if yuh don't mind. Let's have some air here, shall we? See to it, Fishbone, no messin'.' He swung round to Strange, then back to the sleeping man still standing in the shadows. 'Perhaps you gentlemen'll give a hand to clean up.'

'Yuh got a whole sight more than cleanin' up to be done here, fella,' said the sleeping man sidling from the shadows to the glow. 'Name's Goldman, by the way. Frank Goldman.' He

40

eased his weight to one hip and hooked his thumbs in the pockets of his waistcoat. 'Strikes me — ' he began again, raising a slow gaze to Strange.

'Yeah, well, I ain't interested in theorizin', mister. I got passengers to look to, women travellin' single among 'em, and this ain't exactly an attraction on the itinerary. So if yuh don't mind . . . ' Spruce wiped a hand over his sticky face and moved to the body. 'Hell,' he mouthed, glancing quickly at Strange. 'Yuh wouldn't reckon this for — '

'Let's get to it, shall we?' grunted Strange. 'Place is beginnin' to smell.'

They had moved the body across the room to the doorway, wrapped the dead dog in a blanket and gone in search of pails, besoms, cloths and brushes to begin the clean-up when Strange stiffened, called for silence and stepped softly towards the veranda at the growing sound of hoofbeats pounding towards the station.

'Seems like we got company ridin'

in,' said Goldman. 'Busy place, ain't it?' he grinned.

Spruce hissed on a retort, thought better of it and crossed quickly to join Strange, the hoofbeats closing now at a thundering pace, tack swinging and creaking to an eerie jangle.

'Fella either in one helluva hurry, or ain't for stoppin',' murmured Strange, peering into the depths of the thickening night.

'Case yuh ain't noticed,' whispered Spruce at his side, 'we got more than a dead body on our hands. Somebody's scattered the horses. Corral's empty.'

'I noticed,' said Strange. He crossed to the veranda steps at the first blurred image of the approaching rider, saw Fishbone stepping clear of the stage to the open ground, the Winchester tight in his grip, and was already fingering the butt of his Colt when the blaze of a stream of shots ripped like screams across the night; fast, measured shots from the rider slung low in his mount's neck.

'Sonofa-goddam-bitch!' groaned Spruce, and felt his body freeze as if plunged to ice at the sight of Fishbone spinning on his heels where he stood, his head thrown back, rifle flung from his grasp, blood flying from him like a shower of fire sparks before he finally crumpled and thudded to the dirt.

The driver and passengers of the Fort Benham stage were still standing silent and motionless when the hoofbeats had passed and only the echo of them hung in a cloud of night-streaked dust across the loneliness of the Cooney Forks swing station.

5

Francine Devaux stood alone at the far end of the veranda, her gaze flat and unblinking on the silent, starlit night. Pepperthwaite watched her from the shadows, one hand fluttering like a moth to flame at the slip and slide of his spectacles, the other fidgeting in the depths of his frock coat pocket.

Frank Goldman leaned on the door jamb to the station living-room, a cheroot easy in his long, sensitive fingers, his eyes narrowed to dark slits against the curl of smoke.

'And it goes without saying, doesn't it, that the matter will not end there you can rest assured of that,' blustered the colonel's wife, leaning perilessly forward in the ancient chair by the window, the creaks of worn wicker and corset stays merging as if in conversation with themselves. 'It's a positive outrage,' she continued, brushing angrily at a drooping feather from her hat. 'All that trouble in Reuben, then we pick up a perfect stranger out there on the trail — totally unheard of — and then, would you believe, we find ourselves surrounded by dead bodies and the certainty of a madman on the loose, doubtless watching us even as I speak. What next, I ask myself? Well, I will tell you precisely what next — '

'Maybe we should be helping,' murmured Hiram Pepperthwaite, picking specks of dust from his coat lapels.

'Helping?' flared Mrs Fitzsimmons, with a thud of her hands to her lap. 'I will not lift a finger to help, and certainly not to dig graves for dead men, mindful as I am, have always been, of a measure of respect for the deceased. I am a paying passenger, and so, sir, are you.'

'Well, mebbe it'll look a whole lot better come first light,' said Goldman from behind a curling cloud of smoke.

'I fail to see how,' snapped Mrs

Fitzsimmons. 'I see no prospect in first light of satisfactory explanations for what has happened since we had the misfortune to step aboard that stage. There are questions, too many of them, and no answers. What happened here, and why? Who is the man we picked up on the trail, and why did we pick him up? Has he paid? And not least, by no means least, who was the very Devil incarnate who shot Mr Fishbone — why did he, and where, in Heaven's name, is he now? And all that without touching on the subject of just exactly what we are going to do from here on.'

'Mr Wethers'll answer that the minute he and the other fella are through diggin' graves out there,' said Pepperthwaite through a wan grin.

'Oh, really? And what do you suppose he is going to suggest? That we turn about and head back to Reuben? I hope not. I have no wish ... ' Mrs Fitzsimmons stiffened imperiously. 'What have you to say on the matter, young lady?' she asked, her stare tight on Francine Devaux.

The actress waited a moment as if unaware of being addressed, then turned slowly, softly, her eyes round and bright. 'My only concern is to reach Fort Benham as quickly as possible,' she smiled carefully. 'But there are others to consider — Mr Pepperthwaite here, and Mr Goldman.'

'Oh, I'm for pushin' right on, ma'am,' flustered Pepperthwaite. 'Yessir, keep right on goin', and if I can be of any service to yuh personally, Miss Devaux, why, yuh only have to say. Just you name it.'

Goldman coughed and flicked a nub of ash to the floor. 'M'self,' he began with a shrug, 'well, can't say I take kindly to all this death and killin' — t'ain't in my nature to do so — but bein' a man of no particular count to time and place, I'll just pitch in my lot with the majority. Seems like a fair decision.'

'There we are, then,' flounced Mrs

Fitzsimmons, 'we're agreed. We tell Mr Wethers — '

' 'Course,' added Goldman, examining the glow of the cheroot, 'seein' as how the stage driver ain't got nobody ridin' shotgun along of him no more, and in view of what's happened here *and* the fact that some mean-minded sonofabitch has taken it upon himself to scatter the change mounts from the corral, things might not pan out as we're seein' 'em — if yuh get my meanin'.'

'Details, mere details,' huffed the colonel's wife with a dismissive wave of her hand. 'Nothing that cannot be accommodated. As my husband always says: hold to the strategy, accumulate the tactics.'

'Always,' murmured Francine Devaux quietly, her smile gentle on Mrs Fitzsimmons' withering gaze.

'And then, o'course, there's the fast-ridin' gunman we just seen,' added Goldman again.

'You aren't suggestin' he'll follow us,

are you?' frowned Pepperthwaite.

'Well, he ain't gone to all this hell-raisin' trouble for nothin', has he? Ain't come to cold-blooded murder for the fun of it. Fact, I'd figure for him bein' a pretty resolute sorta fella.'

'I'm almost certain I saw him back there in Reuben,' mused Pepperthwaite. 'Couldn't be certain, not in the dark, but there was somethin' . . . '

'A madman,' announced Mrs Fitzsimmons stomping her foot. 'We shall see no more of him, and if we do — '

'I'm sure we can take care of him — one way or another,' said the actress, flicking open her fan.

'Well, yuh can sure trust to me doin' my bit, Miss Devaux,' grinned Pepperthwaite, with a push on his spectacles. 'Why, I remember one time back at Rookstown when I stood face on — '

'Ah,' said Mrs Fitzsimmons creaking expansively to her feet, 'I see the diggers are all through and heading this way. Now we can get to the planning.'

49

'Yuh ain't serious, are yuh?' hissed Spruce Wethers, staring deep into Strange's half-shadowed face, the chill of the night like a flicker of fingers across his shoulders. 'Damnit, t'ain't never been known before, not in my time, anyhow, and I ain't sure there's one line of company regulations would allow it.'

Strange's tight, steady gaze moved watchfully over the darkness beyond the silence of the station, the soft glow of lantern light at his back. 'Yuh got a better idea?' he asked. 'We turn this stage for Reuben at first light and it's two-bits to a marked deck Lenski'll hit us before we gone a mile — mebbe with the Beattie boys along of him if they've got to stirrin'. We stay here and we're a sittin' target come noon. Either way you're puttin' yuh passengers at risk. We go on, me ridin' shotgun, and we'll hit High Point come sundown. Fresh mounts there, so yuh got my word on it

I'll ride on to Fort Benham for help. That way — '

'Yeah, yeah, I hear yuh,' sighed Spruce, 'that way my passengers stay movin' and safe. More to the point, you keep kickin' the dirt from yuh boots. Ain't that the real sum of it?' He grunted. 'Can't deny it, can yuh, and can't say I blame yuh, but, hell, Jim, the risk . . . ' He ran a hand over his chin. 'I lost Fishbone there — been ridin' along of me more years than I recall; darn near a brother — but I laid my word to O'Grady to help yuh. Same time, o'course, I got the outfit and that hotpan of passengers.' He grunted again. ' 'Tween the Devil and a rattler, ain't I?'

'Yuh heard what Mrs Fitzsimmons said: passengers are all for goin' on,' said Strange. 'And she ain't for messin' with.'

'I hear that too!' winced Spruce. 'Hell, do I hear the woman!' He thrust his hands to his pockets. 'Lenski must sure be riled some to get to all this. And

I wouldn't give a spit for him not bein' out there right now. Bet he ain't missed a tick of what we been doin', buryin' poor old Walt and Fishbone. Sonofabitch!' He spat across the dirt. 'No change of horses,' he murmured, scanning the deserted corral. 'Slow goin' to High Point and the team'll be all through by then. Just hope . . . Hell, yuh don't suppose Lenski — ?'

'My reckonin' is he'll wait on joinin' up with Beattie. He'll know we're slowed up. Won't be for goin' it alone now that he's announced himself. We got half an edge there just so long as we keep movin'.'

'Well,' pondered Spruce, 'mebbe we can at that. Easy goin' 'til we reach the draw at Black Mount; four miles through the creek, then steady again 'til Deadstream.'

'So we're goin' on?' said Strange, shifting his gaze to Spruce's face. 'Yuh'll take the chance?'

'Sure, but I want a promise outa you, Jim Strange. Minute we get to High

Point and we fix it for safe passage to Benham, you scoot, fast as yuh can. Don't get me wrong, I'm for what you're tryin' to do to clear yuh name, but while I got the reins to that stage in my hands — '

'Yuh got it, and I shan't claim pay for ridin' shotgun! Now, we got them passengers settled for the night?'

'Miss Devaux, Goldman and Pepperthwaite indoors. Place don't seem to spook 'em none. Mrs Fitzsimmons insists on sleepin' in the stage. Won't set foot inside. Her choice. I'll stand watch to her 'til sun-up.'

'Leave the rest to me,' said Strange.

Spruce Wethers sighed again. 'Knew it the minute I went along with O'Grady back there. Just knew the whole darned stewpot scheme would turn sour. Fishbone reckoned the same, know he did, poor devil. Never knew what hit him. Same goes for Walt. But, hell, there'll come a day . . . '

His voice faded, eyes flashed to Strange's narrowed gaze at the sound of a soft, cringing tread at the rear of the station.

'Lenski!' hissed Spruce.

Strange put a finger to his lips for silence and eased away to the shadows, skirting the lantern glow across the veranda, pausing as he turned towards the deeper darkness of the sprawling bulk to the rear, one hand urging Spruce to stay tight at his back.

They had moved another half-dozen steps when they halted again at the drone of a stifled curse, a stumble, sharp intake of breath, crunch of a boot to dirt. Strange's Colt sat tight in his hand as he tensed, steadied his weight and balance, then moved on, one step slipping gently forward; a pause to listen, eyes narrowing, another step, brisker now so that his spring took him out of Spruce's sight as if swallowed on the night.

Only seconds then before Strange reappeared, Hiram Pepperthwaite's sweat-soaked collar tight in his grip.

'What the hell?' mouthed Spruce,

lending a hand to drag the fellow back towards the lantern glow. 'I thought we'd said as how to stay indoors, damnit,' he croaked as the man shuffled to a dust-stained heap, his spectacles gleaming like fish eyes.

'It's not what yuh think,' he spluttered, pulling at his jacket, dusting the lapels, fingering his collar. 'I thought I heard — '

'Peepin' into Miss Devaux's room,' snapped Strange, holstering his Colt.

'Hell, Mr Pepperthwaite,' said Spruce, 'that ain't no way for a gentleman to behave. Hadn't figured yuh for no Peepin' Tom.'

'I was *not* peepin',' croaked Pepperthwaite, beads of sweat bubbling on his cheeks. 'I heard a noise and thought Miss Devaux might need some help.'

'Lookin' through her window?' frowned Spruce. 'Oh, sure! And did she need some help, or simply *lookin'* to?'

'As it happened, no, she didn't,' said Pepperthwaite, stiffening. 'Mr Goldman was already there. Still is. Go see for yourself.'

'Goldman?' murmured Spruce. 'And what in hell's name is he doin' there?'

'Nothin'. Nothin' remiss, that is. I mean nothin' . . . Damn it, she and Goldman are porin' over some sorta map. Got it spread out there on the bed, pair of 'em, leanin' over it — real intense.' Pepperthwaite brushed savagely at the clinging dust. 'Just that. Nothin' else.'

Spruce's puzzled gaze into Strange's eyes matched the dark uncertainty he saw there.

6

They rolled the stage from Cooney Forks to the trail for Fort Benham at the first blink of light. Spruce, still sickened at the deaths of Fishbone and Walt and the horrors of the bloodbath they had found on arrival at the station, was in no mood for delay or the niceties of an explanation of events.

'Ain't for mullin' over what's happened,' he had said once the passengers were settled in their seats, one hand on the half-closed door. 'No point to it. But seein' as how yuh all for goin' on, that's precisely what we'll do, fast as this worn team here can make it. Swing station at High Point come sundown, if we stay lucky. Should find things a whole sight more civilized there. Meantime, yuh fellow passenger, Mr Strange, has volunteered to ride shotgun along of me.

And grateful I am too.' He had grunted and adjusted his hat self-consciously. 'As for that shootin' here last night — '

'I trust there will be no repetition of that squalid episode, Mr Wethers?' the colonel's wife had huffed to a creak of her corsets and a dance of hat feathers.

'I sure as hell hope not, ma'am — beggin' yuh pardon,' Spruce had nodded. 'Fella's probably long gone by now, but you can be certain he'll figure in my report to the law at Benham.' He had grunted again and shifted his shoulders at an irritating twitch. 'We done the best by the poor souls lost,' he had added quietly. 'Can't do more, not if we're goin' to make Benham on time.'

'Well, you just thank Mr Strange on our behalf, will yuh?' smiled Goldman from a corner-seat. 'Seems to make a habit of travellin' different, don't he? How come he joined the stage back there on the trail, anyhow? He get

58

lost or somethin'?'

'Circumstances,' said Spruce, avoiding Goldman's gaze. 'Just be grateful he did, shall we?'

He had moved to close the door when Francine Devaux had leaned forward and laid a warm, easy hand on his arm. 'I take it we shall be on time at the fort, Mr Wethers?' she had murmured, her eyes brightening to the gentle break of a smile. 'My engagement there is rather special.'

'You can bank on it, ma'am,' Spruce had returned, his gaze softening. 'I ain't never had a stage run late on me yet, and now ain't the time to start. We'll be there.'

And with that, and a final blade-sharp glance from Mrs Fitzsimmons — that might well have been intended as much for Francine Devaux as himself — he had nodded, closed the door and climbed to his driving seat where Jim Strange was already waiting, Fishbone's Winchester cradled across his lap.

'Let's roll the hell out of it!'

Neither Spruce nor Strange had given the grave mounds they passed a second glance. They were still masked in night shadows, anyhow.

★ ★ ★

Hiram Pepperthwaite was making no effort not to stare. In fact, he thought, adjusting his spectacles yet again, he was enjoying the indulgence. And why not? When you had a beautiful woman facing you, no more than a kneecap's distance away, a fella had every right to stare. Such God-given good looks in a body most men would give their horse for were not for being missed. Chance of a lifetime, when you came to reckon it.

And so, he resolved for the twentieth time, he was going to relish every minute of the long, hot, bouncing, dust and dirt-swirling ride to High Point, and not give a damn!

Which was not quite true. He did

give a damn, a whole heap of them, come to it, for the fact that a woman of the looks, character and talent of Francine Devaux should be associating — and deviously too — with a fellow of the cut of Frank Goldman.

Made no sense, did it? Miss Devaux was a star, damnit a near legend in classy circles, with men of wealth and power and high influence practically on their knees for so much as a passing glance from those moon-swept eyes. So how come she was tied in somehow with a scumbag like Goldman? And she was, no question of it; she had been there with him last night, intent as dogs at a bone on that spread map. Another few minutes at the window and he might have got to hearing what they were saying . . . Damn that nosy-parkering Strange!

But what made even less sense in his book was how come they were making no acknowledgement of each other now, when they were seated only feet apart? Not a word, not a glance. Nothing. Total strangers. It just did not figure.

But, then, when he came to thinking it through, it did not figure either that Francine Devaux was here at all. On a cheap-rate stage, on a fly-swarmed trail to a back-of-nowhere place like Fort Benham?

She might well know Colonel Fitzsimmons of old (just how long back?) and she might well be doing him a favour (just what sort of favour?) but Mrs Fitzsimmons was sure as hell not aware of it.

On the other hand . . . Damn it, did it matter? She was here, close as a breath, and, unless he was much mistaken, not one mite averse to his attentions. So why not enjoy it, he resolved again? No saying what this journey might turn up, was there? Hell, it had started eventfully enough!

Even so, it would pay to keep an eye on Goldman. Just one eye, when he could spare the time . . .

* * *

The light was breaking fast, a vast, sun-streaked panorama of scattering clouds to a clear blue sky across the peaks of the distant hill range to the east and an already shimmering haze to the far horizon. But where the shadows still lurked, thin and frail under the gathering light, there were shapes to remind that night and the hidden were not yet done: the tumbling bulges of rocky outcrops, twisted drifts of blown dirt and the gnarled, probing fingers of ancient brush.

Just about anything else you cared to fancy too, thought Spruce, flicking at the reins to hold the stage team's steady pace.

He glanced quickly at Jim Strange riding the sway and bounce with all the ease of a veteran shotgun. 'Yuh see anythin'?' he called above the whip of wind and creaking timbers. 'Seems quiet enough.'

Strange's gaze moved almost casually

over the sweep of land. 'It's quiet,' he answered. 'Lenski's either way back of us waitin' on tyin' himself in with Beattie's guns, or well ahead of us. I'm prayin' on him ridin' our tail.'

Spruce grunted and shouted his encouragement to the team. 'Black Mount in a couple of hours. Take time passin' through there way these horses are respondin'. They're just tired, damn it, same as me!' He shouted again and flicked the reins. 'Yuh given any thought to what Pepperthwaite was tellin' us? Yuh figure for him tellin' it straight?'

'See no reason why he shouldn't. Fella's got a balmy eye for the actress. He wouldn't want her out of his sight for long.'

'And Goldman? Who the hell is he?'

Strange shifted the Winchester. 'That I don't know, and I wouldn't reckon for him bein' too anxious to say.'

Spruce grunted again. 'But him and Miss Devaux, together — t'ain't much of a natural match. And what's with the map, f'Cris'sake? They checkin' on the route or somethin'?'

'Mebbe they were doin' just that.'

'Damn it,' mouthed Spruce, 'of all the mixed bag of beans in Creation, it drops in my lap. And you along of it! And when I come to thinkin' on Fishbone and Walt buried back there, hell, if this ain't the most ... ' He shouted to the team again and spat fiercely. 'Benham can't come fast enough, and that's for sure.'

'Black Mount first,' called Strange, his gaze moving through another sweep of the land.

'And stay prayin'!' murmured Spruce.

* * *

'Resourceful he may be but that is hardly the issue, is it?' Mrs Fitzsimmons leaned to the sway of the stage, blew ferociously at a drooping feather from her hat and heaved her considerable bosoms impatiently. 'Not by my account, it isn't. He might be anybody — of a lawless nature I don't doubt.'

'Well, I wouldn't go quite so far as that,' began Pepperthwaite, mopping at a surge of bubbling sweat. 'I mean, he just might be — '

'A man who joins a stage in the manner of his arrival is certainly up to no good. And it is surely no coincidence that we have since found ourselves at the centre of a singularly bloody train of events.' Mrs Fitzsimmons creaked to the strain of her corsets. 'When my husband comes to hear of this . . . '

'Jim Strange, one-time Sheriff of Franckton, that's who he is,' grunted Goldman from the shadows of his tipped hat. 'Shot a man for no good reason — so they say.'

'There you are, then,' huffed Mrs Fitzsimmons. 'Proves my point.'

'But that don't say he did it,' said Goldman, folding his arms. He sniffed loudly. 'Sure as hell made a mess of somebody back there in Reuben, though, didn't he just? Some shootin'. Real fast.'

'And you mean to say that a murderer is now riding shotgun to this stage?' swelled the woman. 'He's here, on the run no less from his evil doings? Well, really . . . '

'Perhaps a good thing he is,' ventured Pepperthwaite. 'Sorta company we been keepin' of late calls for a gun, faster the better.'

'I do not condone violence, Mr Pepperthwaite, save when it is of a military necessity in the course of the common good. A code my husband has always pursued.'

Francine Devaux smiled delicately. 'Perhaps we *are* the common good,' she said softly.

'Nothin' common about you ma'am,' quipped Hiram Pepperthwaite, mopping again. 'If yuh take my meanin', that is.'

'Why, thank you, Mr Pepperthwaite,' nodded the actress.

Mrs Fitzsimmons stiffened dramatically. 'Speak for yourselves, of course, but I personally wouldn't lay a skim of trust to such a man. No telling where it might lead. Who's to say where he's leading us now? We could be party to the most outrageous scheming.'

'True, ma'am, true,' said Goldman, hunching deeper into his corner-seat. 'Just no sayin' to the ways of folk, is there? But the way I see it . . . well, if we got some gunslingin' scumbag broodin' round our butts, I'm for havin' Mr Strange ridin' shotgun.'

'Same here,' said Pepperthwaite. 'You agree, Miss Devaux?'

'Oh, I'm all for having a man at my side. Frequently.'

Hiram Pepperthwaite sweated and stared wide-eyed. Goldman grunted and grinned, and Mrs Fitzsimmons might have retorted with some pithy comment, save that her words were lost at the sudden bounce, sway and grinding creak of the stage as it slewed to a halt amid the snorting of horses and the jangle of clamouring tack.

It seemed to Hiram Pepperthwaite like forever before the ominous silence was broken and he blinked clear of his obsessive stare.

7

It was a full nerve-shattering minute before Spruce Wethers had the time to stare, and then only in a bewildered disbelief at the chaos across the trail at the mouth of Black Mount that had slewed the stage to a shuddering halt.

'Sonofa-goddamn-bitch!' he moaned, still fighting to hold the team from panic as he took in the mass of scattered landslide rocks strewn ahead of him like the violent wake of a giant's steps. 'What the hell's happened?' He gasped, heaved on the reins and bellowed as the team strained, backed, veered to the left, hoofs pounding dirt, clattering on the looser shale, conscious now of the barrel of Strange's Winchester probing like a finger at the higher reaches of the mountain.

'Hold 'em steady there, Mr Wethers,' shouted Strange, his gaze roving the sunlit ridges. 'We might still have company!'

Spruce heaved again as the team began to settle, heads and manes tossing, wild eyes flashing on the light. 'Don't nobody move!' he yelled, aware then of a stage door swinging open. 'I said don't nobody — '

But too late. Goldman was already out of the stage and on his feet, his gaze following the ranging probe of the rifle. 'Yuh see anythin', mister?' he called. 'Anybody up there?'

'Not now there ain't,' said Strange, dropping from his seat to the trail, 'but there was, and not so long back.'

'Give me two guesses,' quipped Goldman. 'The lead-happy gunslinger we had for company last night? I'll bet! Been busy, ain't he?'

Strange merely grunted as he moved away to the head of the team, murmuring softly to the horses as he went.

'I might've known we hadn't seen the last of that scum,' croaked Spruce,

71

gathering loose reins in his grip. 'So much for him sittin' on our butts, eh? The hell he is!'

'Am I to assume there will be some delay, Mr Wethers?' snapped the colonel's wife, leaning like a feather-hatted bear through the open door.

'Yes, ma'am,' drawled Spruce irritably, 'you most certainly can!'

'Then might I suggest — '

'No, ma'am, yuh can't! Yuh just get y'self back in there and stay put. Same goes for you, Mr Goldman. Folk ridin' my stage are under my protection. I ain't for havin' heads blown off, if yuh don't mind.'

'Mite late to get worryin' on that score,' sneered Goldman, still watching the ridges. 'Should've figured for the fella not givin' up that easy. Must've been here at first light.' He pointed to the highest of the jagged line of ridge. 'Enough loose rock up there for him to only have to breathe to set it rollin'.'

'I got eyes. I can see,' croaked Spruce.

'Then yuh'd best get to seein' just how —'

'Hold it there,' ordered Strange, stepping back to the stage. 'Ain't no point in rantin' on. We're here, and what we see is what we got.' He crooked the Winchester's stock to his armpit. 'Any chance of skirtin' round this, Mr Wethers?' he asked calmly.

'Goin' to have to,' croaked Spruce. 'Can't go through it, or over it.' He scratched his chin thoughtfully. 'Only chance we got is the one-horse track to the south side of Deadstream. Slow goin' even for a fresh team. With this outfit . . . Well, I wouldn't set no store by it.'

'Perhaps we should turn back,' called Pepperthwaite from the other side of the stage.

'No!' blurted Goldman, flaring for an instant. 'I mean, no, not if there is another way. Be a real waste, wouldn't it, havin' come this far?'

'You in a hurry or somethin'?' frowned Spruce.

'Not particularly,' shrugged Goldman, adjusting the lapels of his coat. 'Just that I ain't for backin' off. Fella out there don't spook me none, and 'sides we got Miss Devaux and Mrs Fitzsimmons back there anxious to get to Benham soon as possible.'

'We're all going to get to Fort Benham,' said Spruce, stiffening, his eyes gleaming.

'Well, I'm glad to hear it,' grinned Goldman. 'That's the spirit, ain't it, Mr Strange? Just keep right on goin', eh? Yuh'd know about that, wouldn't yuh?'

Strange's gaze had darkened in a steady stare when Mrs Fitzsimmons leaned from the stage door again, one hand settled firmly on her hat. 'Will somebody kindly tell what is happening?' she bellowed. 'Mr Wethers, I hold you responsible.'

'We're goin' on, ma'am,' answered Spruce. 'Takin' the track south.'

'Are you sure of the way? Do you have a map?'

Spruce turned to Strange and Goldman. 'Map?' he mouthed sarcastically. 'Now just what would I be doin' with such a thing? You have a map, Mr Goldman?'

Goldman hesitated, then shrugged. 'Ain't never seen one,' he muttered.

'No, ma'am,' called Spruce to the colonel's wife. 'Don't have no map. Don't need one.'

'Well, I just hope you know where you're going,' said the woman, easing back to her seat with a defiant creak and thud. 'My husband always sets great value on a correctly drawn map,' she huffed, eyeing Francine Devaux and Pepperthwaite like a hawk. 'I don't suppose either of you has such a thing? Miss Devaux?'

'No, not at all,' said the actress with the merest flicker of her fingers over her dress. 'I generally know my way around well enough,' she smiled.

'I'm sure you do, my dear.' said Mrs Fitzsimmons, planting a drooping hat feather into place. 'I'm sure you do.'

'So let's get to rollin', shall we?' shouted Spruce, taking the strain of the reins. 'Got some miles to close on before Deadstream. Yessir!'

Hiram Pepperthwaite polished his spectacles vigorously and went back to staring. Francine Devaux was a beautiful woman, he thought, relaxing to the grind of timbers, squeak of wheels and scrambling hoofs. A fine actress too. No role too daunting, none too minor. Always believable — even when she was lying.

* * *

The sun was high, the air thick with heat and flies, the horizon a haze of shimmering light by the time Spruce and Strange had the stage swung to the new trail south and the one-horse track they would follow to Deadstream.

'This pace and no faster,' announced Spruce once the team had settled to a steady beat and wheels were rolling easy. 'Horses won't take no more. We

76

water up first chance we get. Meantime . . . ' He had paused a moment to glance to left and right. 'Hell, don't have to say it, do I? Just don't miss a thing, yuh hear? First fly that gets too close, shoot it! And I ain't foolin' neither.' He had grunted moodily and spat. 'Yuh reckon for Lenski bein' well ahead by now?' he had asked. 'That episode back there just a warnin', remindin' us he's still with us?'

'He won't be for sittin' it out in this heat. He's done enough for now. Next chance he gets'll be at High Point.'

'Well, I just hope Charlie Gills out there ain't sleepin' on the job. High Point ain't the best of stations, and Charlie surely ain't for takin' no prizes when it comes to runnin' it. Go down a whole lot easier than Walt.' Spruce had swung the sweat from his face, and spat again. 'Goldman's a liar, ain't he?' he had growled suddenly, as if stumbling into the thought. 'The hell he's never seen a map! What I want to know is just what he and the actress woman were studyin' back there at Cooney.'

To which, thought Strange, remaining silent, Spruce might have added: 'And why?' But there was enough for him to ponder at this moment fathoming the vague trail, holding the team to its pace — without the hindrances of Goldman and Francine Devaux. They would wait — for now.

Spruce would have been a sight more concerned with the news that it was as certain as noon to night that Lenski was not riding alone, not if the tracks Strange had noted leaving the chaos at the mount were anything to go by.

Somewhere, at some time since the killings at Cooney, Lenski had joined up with another rider. By chance, or had one of Beattie's men been lurking look-out for where the gunfighter might head? Either way, it seemed the price standing to the shooting of Jim Strange was still there and worth going to a heap of trouble and effort for the lifting.

But that was hardly a matter to bother Spruce Wethers with right now. He would simply get to fretting.

8

Sheriff Frank O'Grady had good reason to remember that high summer morning. Not for the pitch and roll of a stage, the straining snorts of a tired team; nor for the slips and slides of a long lost trail, the shimmers of heat, the depth of tight shadows.

He would remember noon on that morning for the fact that at a quarter past it he regained consciousness.

He came to slowly, painfully, his muscles and limbs still pounding to the beating he had taken at the hands of the four men who had stepped quietly, smilingly into his office soon after sun-up. Men he had known well enough; ordinary, easygoing, hardworking fellows from out the Beattie ranch. Regular townmen when they had dollars in their pockets and a fancy for spending. But never no trouble. They

80

came, spent their money and left. Men of habit. You could read them like an open book.

So how come they had turned to a blank page and decided to write their own chapter of events?

He winced and groaned as he struggled from the cluttered, blood-smeared floor, his hands settling like manacles for support on his desk. Be a help if he could see straight through the swollen slits that passed for eyes.

He ran a dirt-pitted tongue over his slanted lips where there seemed to be about as many ridges and clefts as you would find in a day's mountain riding; winced again at the gaps in his gums where teeth had once gleamed, and slumped exhausted into his chair, his mind reeling through a turmoil of sounds and images.

'Mr Beattie ain't happy,' the spokesman for the four had announced bluntly as the men slouched into the office. 'Seems like yuh been extendin' yuh authority somewhat. T'ain't written as how yuh gotta right to aid killers gettin' clear of bein' brought to law.' He had run the tip of a gnarled, grubby finger over the surface of O'Grady's desk. 'Guess yuh know who I'm referrin' to?' he had added darkly.

Instinct had warned O'Grady then that there was going to be no discussion of the matter: Moran Beattie had heard of the shooting of Reisner, the escape of Lenski and, somehow, from some lily-livered quarter, of the smuggling out of town to join the stage at Spencer Bend of Jim Strange. Heard, pronounced his version of judgement, and sent in the warders to mete out the punishment. Nothing so final as an execution, of course. Too messy, too much explaining wasting valuable time.

'Put Mr Beattie to a whole lot of trouble,' the man had continued. 'Even had to send his younger son, Virgil, out into them wild lands back of Cooney Forks. And now he figures he might just have to ride out there his very self to see the issue settled to his satisfaction. That's a real pain to him this time of year. So yuh see, he ain't one bit happy, and when Mr Beattie ain't happy, well . . . '

That, O'Grady had thought, would be about the sum of the indictment. These boys were not for slouching too long when doubtless they had been given money to spend as they saw fitting across at the Sweetcall.

Best he could do, he had resolved, would be to send at least one of them to the bar with an already splitting head.

The beating had been thorough, systematic, no-holds barred and fast, so that within eight minutes of the men entering his office they were all through, dusting down and ready to leave. And they had gone almost as quietly as they had arrived. Three of them at least were still smiling.

O'Grady shifted, hissing at the stabs of pain, the dead, leaden weight of his limbs, and eased his arms across the desk, his blurred, blood-netted vision swimming on the shaft of light from the office window.

Town seemed quiet enough now, he thought. Maybe Beattie's sidekicks had drunk up and left, or staggered off some place to sleep it off. No point in raising the strength to find out; let them go, report back to Beattie that the sheriff had been taught a tough lesson and would be no further problem.

Too right, he winced, shifting again, no problem — at least not hereabouts in Reuben. But out there, wherever Jim Strange had wandered, might be another matter. Damn it, somebody had to stand to the fellow, and seeing as how he had come this far, to this state, was there another option? Just give it time, shot or two of that whiskey he had stored back of the office, a decent wash, clean clothes, and he would be all set.

Even so, it would be a long two hours into the late afternoon before Sheriff

O'Grady was on his feet, standing steady, seeing clearly and confident enough to make the first moves towards hitting the trail for Fort Benham. And by then the cuts, bruises, pounded body and numbed limbs were lost in his growing anger, disgust and determination.

He hardly felt a thing when he crossed to the rifle cabinet and selected the two most trusted Winchesters from the rack.

* * *

'Do you suppose we shall be near anything like civilization by nightfall?' Mrs Fitzsimmons threw out the question as if discarding the last portion of a poor meal, adjusted the fit of her gloves and glared for attention.

'Well,' began Pepperthwaite, rescuing his spectacles against another grinding bounce of the stage, 'that depends. Way I see it, we must be runnin' some hours behind schedule. On the other hand, we're makin' good progress. At least it seems like we are. Not that I'm any real judge, o'course.'

'Yes or no?' snapped the colonel's wife, turning her attention to Goldman. 'What do you think?'

'Couldn't say,' grunted Goldman from behind his tipped hat. 'I leave it to them doin' the drivin'.'

Mrs Fitzzimmons huffed and stiffened. 'Miss Devaux, you seem to have an opinion on most things. What do you say?'

'I imagine Mr Wethers is giving the matter his full attention,' said the actress, smiling carefully. 'As Mr Pepperthwaite says, we are making progress.'

Pepperthwaite sighed, Mrs Fitzsimmons creaked. 'Perhaps,' she said haughtily, 'but without a map let me remind you. Treacherous country without some guidance, I would suggest. No saying where some of these tracks might lead.'

'That feller, Strange, ain't no fool,'

murmured Goldman. 'He won't be for wastin' time.'

'Ah, yes, Mr Strange.' Mrs Fitzsimmons slapped her hands into her lap. 'We shall need to discuss what to do about him. Can't have such a man roaming the country at will. Highly dangerous. I shall need to consult my husband on his fate.'

Goldman pushed his hat clear of his face. 'I reckon not, ma'am. Ain't no man — not even your husband — gets to settlin' Jim Strange's fate, unless, o'course, he's spoilin' for trouble. I reckon your husband would see it that way too.'

'Gerald has never shirked his responsibilities, military or civil. It is not in his code.'

'That mebbe so, ma'am,' smiled Goldman, 'but yuh should know that Mr Strange has his own code, and I wouldn't figure for it — '

The stage lurched violently. Wheels screamed, timbers threatened to splinter. Horses snorted, tack jangled.

'What in the name of — ' spluttered Pepperthwaite as his glasses slid to his knees.

'Stay right where yuh are, folks,' yelled Spruce. 'And I mean stay!'

A sudden, thickening silence descended as if rolled into place. Hiram Pepperthwaite blinked and sweated. Goldman glanced anxiously at Francine Devaux whose eyes in their stare began to darken. The colonel's wife ran her fingers over the feathers in her hat.

'What has happened?' hissed Pepperthwaite. 'Why have we stopped?'

'We got company,' said Strange, appearing at the window on the shadowed side of the stage. 'Trackin' us a mite too close for comfort.'

'Not another free-riding passenger!' groaned Mrs Fitzsimmons.

'No, ma'am, I wouldn't reckon this fella to be lookin' for a ride. One dead body more like.'

'The gunman?' croaked Pepperthwaite. 'The one we saw back at Cooney?'

Strange eased closer. 'He ain't lookin' for none of you, take my word on it. But if yuh happen to be in the way . . . So yuh stay tight. Yuh got that? Just don't move.'

'Yuh see him?' said Strange, joining Spruce in the deepest of the shadows.

'Still up there, same place we first spotted him. That line of crags. He's watchin', yuh bet on it. But t'ain't Lenski, I'll swear to that.'

Strange grunted and scanned the line of seemingly empty rocks.

'So what yuh reckon?' asked Spruce. 'We push on?'

'Too risky,' murmured Strange, still watching the rocks. 'Couldn't make the pace over this ground, and if he gets to pepperin' lead this way . . . ' His gaze narrowed. 'We take him out.'

'Yuh mean we start shootin'?' hissed Spruce. 'Hell, we do that and there'll be a bloodbath down here.'

'Yuh stay outa sight, and keep them passengers calm. Leave the fella up there to me.'

'Yeah, well you just make it fast, yuh hear?' swallowed Spruce. 'We're an hour short of makin' the trail to High Point, and I ain't for trundlin' this outfit at night.' He swallowed again and began to sweat. 'Supposin' that scumbag up there ain't alone? Supposin' Lenski's with him?'

'Just supposin',' said Strange, slipping from Spruce's side to disappear among the rocks.

'I am!' groaned Spruce to no one.

9

The stance, the height, set of the shoulders, angle of the broad-brimmed hat, loose, easy handling of the Winchester — there had been no mistaking them. No need for a sight of the fellow's face. One glance had been enough. Virgil Beattie had teamed with Lenski and was here now, strutting the rim of the high rock drift above the one-horse trail south of Deadstream like a man in a hurry to be done with the business and heading back to town.

Strange licked his lips, squatted deeper into the cover of the rocks and narrowed his gaze on the slope to the rim. No sight of the fellow in the last few minutes, not since he had seen the stage grind to a halt, watched the hesitation in Spruce Wethers' hands — take a grip and push on, or wait and let Strange do the hunting? — and seen the one-time sheriff slip away to the shadows.

But he would be waiting, bet your life on it, thought Strange, edging to the next lift of cover; giving it time, distance, until from somewhere up there, once he had the range, he would let rip with a volley of fire that would spray the slope like rain.

That was Virgil's way: fast, hot-headed, arrogant; not a deal of reckoning to subtlety; nothing smart or shrewd.

It suited, mused Strange, shifting again to drop behind a sprawl of boulders. Only edge worth having against a gunman with fast killing in mind was in knowing he would stay true to his mould. And Virgil was clear cut from his father's ways and thinking. Beattie power-ruled, whoever, whatever straddled his path.

He grunted, waited a moment and moved on, careful to stay with the shadows, the tightest cover, angling his climb from left to right and back again, one eye on his footholds, the other on the high rim.

So, he pondered, pausing to watch, listen, catch his breath, it had come down to the baron sending out his youngest to settle the issue. Beattie must be getting impatient; irritated that Reisner and Lenski had failed him, suspicious of Lenski's motives from here on, but seeing in a lone stage with Strange aboard the opportunity for a settlement that few would come to question. Stage had been hit by marauding raiders, the story would go, and if that meant taking out all riding the Reuben — Fort Benham line on that day . . . Beattie power-ruled!

But where was Lenski right now? Up there with Virgil? Lurking in the background, a second gun to hand if things got awkward, or would the young gunslinger have figured for the longer odds of riding on to High Point?

Strange gritted his teeth, wiped the sweat from his neck and eased on, conscious now of coming into range of

Beattie's Winchester. How long before the first spitting hail of lead? How long before Beattie lifted those arrogant shoulders from his cover? No way of knowing from here where he might have holed-up, not until his confidence got the better of him and he made a move.

Strange settled, breathing easy, his gaze scanning the skies, where already the light was beginning to fade against the onset of dusk and the sweep of deepening shadows. He glanced hurriedly back to the stage, a black silent bulk below him, where nothing moved save in the toss of one of the team's heads. Spruce would be counting the minutes, sweating out the prospects, fretting on his passengers, rueing the day Jim Strange had ridden into Reuben and passed through the batwings of the Sweetcall Bar.

A movement. Slip of a disturbed rock, no more than pebble size, shift of a shadow that had no good cause to move. Silence. Another sliding rock, tell-tale scrape of boot leather seeking a hold. Ahead and to the right. Beattie's patience was running thin.

Strange reached softly for the feel of his Colt, lifted it from the holster, weighed it carefully in his grip, winced at the ache in his knees, took a deep breath and inched away to the left.

Cover was still holding, but he needed to be higher, closer to the rim, put the glow of the evening light at his back. He had crawled on another three yards when the first shots splintered, skimmed and shattered across the rocks above him.

'Got the measure of yuh, Strange,' mocked Beattie behind a tittering, child-like giggle. 'I ain't for draggin' this out. Yuh goin' to step clear, or yuh want for this to get messy? Way I'm seein' it they could be scrapin' yuh off those rocks there soon enough. What'll it be?'

Strange stayed silent, unmoving, gaze tight on the shadow that had moved.

'Sight quicker to show yourself at

Franckton, weren't yuh? Didn't waste no time then, eh? Couldn't get to the thick of it fast enough. Wild with it. I seen it all.'

A hawk, splatter of spittle.

'Still sickens me to see my brother, Arran, goin' down like that, and him not full clothed neither. That the way of it with you, Strange, yuh take out the easy meat first? T'ain't much to say for a man wearin' the badge of the law, is it? Wouldn't sleep easy along of that.'

Shift of a foot, flicker of the shadow.

'Well, we sure as hell come to a reckonin' now, ain't we? Doin' this for Arran, yuh know, and my pa back there. Only fittin', ain't it, like that Good Book says: eye for an eye? Can't argue that.'

No hint of Lenski up there, thought Strange, licking at a prickle of sweat. Beattie was alone, talking himself out, but how much of a target had he really got? More to the point, how much more had he got to say?

'Yuh hearin' all this?' snapped the

man ahead of another scrape of boot. 'Time's runnin' out for yuh.'

'Yuh got this all wrong, Virgil,' called Strange, crawling another yard into cover. 'Yuh know well as I do whose lead it was took out Arran. Not mine. Damnit, yuh were close enough!'

'Don't mess with me, Strange. This ain't the time and place. I got more pressin' matters.'

'Yuh bet yuh have!' clipped Strange, his gaze narrowing on the growing shadow. 'Yuh got that sonofabitch Lenski to look to for a start. Your pa still goin' to pay up, or yuh doin' the dirty work for him? Best get it sorted if yuh want my advice.'

'I don't want nothin' from you, fella, 'ceptin' to see yuh dead!' snarled Beattie. 'And right now!'

Strange was moving now, faster, silently, scrambling like an insect over the rocks, hands and feet fighting for holds, eyes still watching the shadow, waiting for its reach to thicken. 'Suit y'self,' he croaked. 'Only trying to be helpful. Me, I wouldn't trust the scumbag — ' And then he was clear of the cover, on his feet, legs tightening for balance, his Colt fixed and steady in his grip.

Beattie swung round from his hide between boulders, the Winchester barrel probing but even then ranged too high for the shots that blazed from it to do more than spit harmlessly into space above Strange's head.

Beattie cursed, fumbling on his grip, sweat lathering his brow, beading like pebbles across his eyes.

'Never did get the hang of handlin' a piece, did yuh?' grinned Strange. 'Always relyin' on the other fella bein' too slow. Bad habit, Virgil. Yuh should've been broken of it long back.'

Strange's words were no more than muffled sounds behind the roar of his Colt as the lead raged and Virgil Beattie fell back, at first slowly, like a puppet collapsing on slack lines, the Winchester drooping in his hands, eyes widening, flickering, glazing, lips mouthing on croaked groans and moans, and then, with hardly a murmur, to a crumpling heap, shoulders crunched up against the rock.

'Damn fool,' murmured Strange, eyes narrowed, still unblinking on the drifting gunsmoke.

He waited no more than seconds before holstering the Colt, turning his back on the body and making his way down the rocky, shadow-shafted slope to the stage, barely conscious of the faces watching him, or the silence that had seemed to creep in like a nervous onlooker slipping from hiding.

★　★　★

'Hell!' groaned Spruce, heaving the team to a steadier pace over the twisting track. 'Did you have to?'

Jim Strange stared ahead at Spruce's side and rocked the Winchester into place across his lap. 'Not a deal of choice when a fella's for havin' yuh dead,' he grunted.

'But Virgil Beattie, f'Cris'sake,' groaned Spruce again. 'Yuh got the vaguest notion of how the old man's goin' to take this? He's goin' to be in one helluva bull-whipped fury, and spittin' it right down our throats! How's that grab yuh, mister?'

'I'll live with it,' murmured Strange.

'You might, but me, them folk back there . . . And, damnit, we still got Lenski to face!' Spruce slapped the reins and cursed. 'How in the name of tarnation did I ever get into this?'

Strange relaxed and scanned the dusk-cloaked land. 'Beats me,' he said quietly, 'why a map would be worth lyin' for. Real odd.'

Spruce Wethers simply groaned and went back to driving the team. High Point before full dark, he thought, raising his eyes to the heavens on a deeper curse.

10

The gathering darkness, the sounds of the creaking stage, roll of wheels, jangling tack and pounding hoofs heightened to a haunting resonance in the early night, had cocooned the four passengers riding the line to Fort Benham in a silence they all seemed reluctant to leave.

Frank Goldman had slumped to his familiar sleeping position in the corner seat, but was not sleeping; not even dozing. His eyes were alive and watchful beneath the tipped brim of his hat, and the steady, rhythmic tap of a forefinger on his knee was proof enough of the thinking spinning quietly behind them.

Hiram Pepperthwaite was no longer enthralled by simply staring. He had seen all he could safely handle of the alluring Francine Devaux; now it was time to fathom the intrigue. Just where, he was pondering, was she keeping that map? Somewhere on her person, had to be, and just what precisely was it a map of? And why, damn it, share it with Goldman?

It was just not in character, he reasoned, for a woman of her standing and character to be involved in something so . . . he was about to think, so 'mysterious', but maybe he meant underhand. Of course, he similarly reasoned, it posed as much of a problem to fathom why she was travelling alone — if, in fact, she was. Supposing she and Goldman . . . What the hell, he was getting to wandering!

Say one thing for her, though, nothing ruffled her. All that shooting back there, and she had never so much as batted an eyelid.

It required stomach, Mrs Fitzsimmons had resolved between the grinding of the stage and the creaking of her corsets; bone-hard guts as her husband would have put it more dramatically at one of his operations briefings.

Common gunfighting; no other description for it. Two men displaying the most primitive of instincts, and here she was caught at the very heart of it. Gerald would have something to say about that! And so would she, the very minute they pulled into High Point. Meanwhile, there were guts to be shown and some careful tactics to be exercised. Somebody had to take control before the enigmatic Mr Strange got completely out of hand.

No point in looking to Pepperthwaite. He was oblivious to time and place and obviously obsessed with the actress hussy, Francine Devaux. And she, of course, would be quite useless in a crisis. Surprising that Gerald had graced her with the favour of a visit to Benham. As for Goldman, well really, he was a case of almost total inertia. Just who or what was he, for heaven's sake?

So, she thought, as she braced herself

against the roll of the stage, she would have to take an initiative. Nothing else for it.

'I take it we shall have access to the law once we reach High Point?' she announced, breaking the long silence abruptly.

Three sets of eyes turned to her: Pepperthwaite as if hearing the tread of a ghost; Francine Devaux with a sudden gleam of curiosity; Goldman slowly without disturbing his hat.

'A sheriff, marshal or something,' added Mrs Fitzsimmons. 'The shooting back there cannot be overlooked. Somebody should be brought to book — as indeed should *somebody* for this entire fiasco.'

'Shouldn't meddle if I were you, ma'am,' grunted Goldman from the corner.

'I would hardly describe standing witness to murder as meddling,' huffed the woman.

'Fair fight,' said Goldman. 'Fella defended himself. Ain't no law against that. Lucky for us he did.'

'Well, I hardly see that!' snapped Mrs Fitzsimmons, adjusting the perch of her hat.

'Whoever it was skulkin' in them rocks weren't doin' it for his health, ma'am. True, he appears to have had Mr Strange as his prime target, but supposin' it had gone the other way. Supposin' it was Strange stiffenin' to crow meat out there. Why, no sayin' as to what his killer might've gotten to, maybe with others along of him. Could've been a carnage — with you ladies there catchin' the worst of it.'

Francine Devaux shifted uncomfortably, while Mrs Fitzsimmons stiffened.

'He's right, lady,' said Pepperthwaite tentatively. 'Could've been just like that. I heard of such things. What about that time back at Morgan Town when them Dolman boys rode in? Weren't a woman who wasn't — '

'Yes, yes, Mr Pepperthwaite,' sighed Mrs Fitzsimmons with a wave of gloved hand, 'I know all about Morgan Town, but that instance and this have little in common.'

'Save killin' and rape,' grunted Goldman again. 'That common enough for yuh?'

'Well,' began the colonel's wife, but for once fell pointedly silent, her hands stern in her lap.

'I'm just for makin' it to High Point,' grinned Pepperthwaite, beginning to sweat. 'I guess we'll get to sortin' things there. Decent meal, a wash and a bed for the night won't come amiss, that's for sure. What yuh say, Miss Devaux, you for a sight of home comforts? Bet yuh are at that, eh?'

Hiram Pepperthwaite's enthusiasm for the protective gesture had brought his hand to rest instinctively on the actress's knee — a move he might have thought better of on another occasion, but not in this instance as the tips of his fingers came to rest on the edge of a shape beneath the woman's dress that seemed oddly out of place.

Something folded. Something that

might for all the world have been very like a map.

Francine Devaux's stare into his eyes as the hand came slowly away from her knee might have seemed accommodating.

Or was it devouring?

★ ★ ★

'Hallelujah, thank the Lord, if that ain't Charlie Gills, moth-eaten as an old shirt and a sight for sore eyes, I do declare!'

Spruce Wethers croaked a dust-baked whoop as he swung the team and stage from the pitted southern trail to the swing station at High Point. Lantern glow from the windows and sprawling veranda broke across the shadows like blades; horses curious to greet the night arrivals gathered at the corral fence; a dog began to bark, another to prance anxiously at Charlie's side as he raised his arms in welcome.

'Ain't I just relieved to see you!' he

called, stepping forward to the swirling dust clouds. 'Don't rightly know what the hell's goin' on round here, but t'ain't one mite to my likin'.'

He removed his hat and waved it against the dust, his eyes squinting for a closer view. 'Where's Fishbone? The old buzzard finally takin' to his bed or somethin'?' He blinked and squinted again. 'And just where in tarnation yuh been all this time? Yuh givin' them folk yuh got loaded a tour of the territory? T'ain't like you . . . ' It was a full ten seconds then before Charlie could find his voice between parched swallows. 'Say, ain't that . . . The hell it is! What in creation is Jim Strange doin' ridin' shotgun? Damn me if it don't seem like the whole world is goin' chuckle-headed!'

'Long story,' said Spruce settling the reins as the team lathered, snorted and steamed to a halt. 'Look to the passengers and the horses, and we'll get to explainin'.'

'And there's a heap of that to be

done,' groaned Charlie moving to the stage door. 'Beginnin' with how it is I got some gun-snappy sonofabitch ridin' round this spread like there's a hoe-down comin' up.' He pulled the door open with a flourish. 'And while we're at it — '

'Ah ah!' boomed Mrs Fitzsimmons descending to the dirt with a thrust of bosoms, waft of lavender and swirl of hat-feathers, 'the smell of cooking! Civilization!' She turned on Charlie with the suddenness of a hawk spotting prey. 'No dead bodies, I presume?' Charlie's mouth dropped open. 'Good,' smiled the colonel's wife. 'It will make a welcome change! This way, people,' she beckoned, creaking majestically to the veranda. 'We appear to have reached safety!'

11

There had still been an hour to full nightfall when Sheriff Frank O'Grady had ridden into the haunted, shadow-filled sprawl of Cooney Forks and been welcomed by ghosts.

The silence, the emptiness, graves newly dug and marked, the smell of death on the balmy evening air — he had needed no more than the few minutes spent gazing over the spread to imagine what had happened here and see the evidence of it clear before his eyes.

'Lenski,' he had murmured, holding his mount steady at the far end of the deserted corral.

His grunt, his last hurried glances, moment of concentration on the darkening trail ahead, had been all he had left to the mournful place before riding on, swinging sharply to the eastern trail to skirt Black Mount on the mountain route to High Point. Be hard going, he reckoned, but worth the effort if it meant getting to the stage before Lenski and the Beattie boys closed for the kill.

Sun-up and not a minute later, he resolved, wincing at a sudden stab of pain somewhere deep in his back.

Fifteen minutes later, Cooney Forks had slid from sight to the darkness to which it belonged and Sheriff O'Grady was long gone.

★ ★ ★

'So there, yuh got it in one,' said Charlie Gills, slapping his near toothless gums round a wad of chewing baccy. 'That fellow, Lenski, is rovin' hereabouts like a lost coyote. Been about most of the day. Ridin' close in watchin', passin' on. And now I know why. Waitin' on you, ain't he? Figurin' on joinin' up with the Beattie boys again and hittin' the stage. No witnesses, and Jim Strange dead.'

He spat a long fount of spittle. 'Goin' to be one helluva sight disappointed, ain't he, and about as friendly as a spooked rattler when he gets to figurin' what's happened? Yuh want my advice?' he asked, his old man's gaze tight on Jim Strange's face. 'Goin' to get it, anyhow. One of yuh gets to Fort Benham faster than forked lightning. Yuh goin' to need help here time that Beattie mob rolls in. Fresh mount waitin' on yuh right now. So who's it goin' to be?'

Spruce Wethers sighed tiredly. 'Damn it, I should've known — '

'Yeah, well mebbe yuh should,' said Charlie, 'but now ain't the time for it. It's doin' that's goin' to count, and seein' as how this whole tangle of a mess seems to be sittin' at your door, Jim Strange, I reckon on you bein' the one for Benham. Yuh figure?'

Strange shifted his weight to one hip where he lounged in the shadowed corner of the veranda, leaned back and folded his arms. 'S'right, Charlie,' he said softly. 'Couldn't have put it better. I ride.'

'Now just yuh hold up there,' blustered Spruce. 'I gotta say in this. I got an outfit and passengers and a contract to hold to, and I ain't never needed no nursin' nowheres. Stage leaves Reuben and it gets to Benham. That's the way of it. Talk of callin' in boot-squeakin' military ain't necessarily to my likin'.'

'Yuh have a choice?' frowned Charlie.

'Sure I do. Brought the stage this far, ain't I? Here to Two Knees Canyon, fast trail west . . . make Benham in a day and a half.'

'Well, mebbe yuh should get to askin' yuh passengers how far they're prepared to stretch their necks,' spat Charlie. 'Could be they ain't for no hell-for-leather race stayin' a spit ahead of hot lead. 'Specially them ladies there — and 'specially the colonel's wife. Yuh lose out on her, Spruce Wethers, and they'll hang yuh, sure as fate.'

'Supposin' — ' began Strange.

'Supposin' nothin',' snapped Spruce. 'Yuh free to ride out whenever yuh like, Jim. That was the deal I struck with O'Grady: get yuh clear of Reuben, then you're on your own. And so yuh are. Right now! And you, Charlie, will be ridin' shotgun along of me come first light. If Lenski and the Beattie scum want Jim Strange, well, let 'em go get him. Pains me to say it, Jim, but that's the way of it. Damn it, that's the *only* choice I got!'

Strange slid his arms to his sides. 'Either way, it seems I ride.'

'Oh, sure, sure,' protested Charlie, 'and just what are we going to tell Lenski when he breaks cover at first light — that yuh couldn't wait on him and rode out? Yuh want for us to give him directions, f'Cris'sake? And what if he ain't of a mood to thank us kindly and move on? What if he and whoever's ridin' along of him, reckons on us standin' witness to murder; what if he's lookin' for retribution wherever it shows its head? Hell, there ain't goin' to be a deal of us worth sayin' words over, is there? We already lost Fishbone; Walt Petcham's pushin' weeds back there at Cooney. What say we get to diggin' now?'

'Ain't no cause for talk like that,' said Spruce. 'All I'm sayin' is — '

'Said a sight too much by my reckonin'.'

The voice came from the shadows at the far end of the veranda; flat, measured tones, unhurried, few words but chosen carefully and no mistaking the threat in them.

'Who the devil — ?' croaked Spruce, spinning on his heel to the sound.

'Who's that? Who's there?' grunted Charlie.

Strange stayed silent, his gaze narrowed to dark, probing slits.

'It's all talk, anyhow,' grinned Goldman stepping to the fringe of lantern light, a Colt firm, balanced and menacing in his grip. 'Ain't nobody goin' nowhere, not yet, not 'til I say so.'

'Just what the hell yuh sayin' there?' snapped Spruce, shuffling a half step forward.

'Easy, easy,' droned Goldman, the Colt twitching a fraction. 'I ain't for using this piece unnecessary, which ain't to say I won't. Perhaps Mr Strange would slip that gunbelt to the floor?'

Strange obliged and stood loose.

'You outa your mind there, fella?' said Charlie, slapping the chewing baccy round his mouth. 'Gettin' spooked some, that it? Hell, man, all we doin' here is figurin' on how best we're goin' to get you folks to Benham. What yuh here for, ain't it?'

Goldman's grin widened. 'Not quite — in fact, not by a long shot. But that ain't your concern right now.'

'The hell it ain't!' scoffed Charlie. 'Fella levels a piece on my station and he can expect — '

Charlie had not expected the reaction to his move to step closer, certainly not anticipated the sudden roar and spit of the single shot that buried lead deep in his shoulder, spinning him back to the station wall with a thud behind his groan as he slumped to the floor.

'That's just to show I mean business,' growled Goldman, one eye on Spruce as he knelt to Charlie's side, the other on Strange with the Colt held steady. 'So no more messin', eh?'

The door space filled with the feather-hatted bulk of Mrs Fitzsimmons, Pepperthwaite sweating at her shoulder, until Francine Devaux spat out her orders with a wave of her own levelled gun. 'Inside! Get back!'

'This is an outrage!' bellowed the colonel's wife, pushing Pepperthwaite aside as she swirled into the living-room. 'What on earth is goin' on?'

'I have a feelin',' began Pepperthwaite, rescuing his spectacles, 'we might just have . . . ' He stared into Francine Devaux's icy gaze. 'The map, damn it, the map . . . '

'Shut it!' snapped the woman.

'Ease up there, all of yuh,' clipped Goldman. 'Clean up that fella there and get him indoors, then yuh all settle down, yuh hear? And no heroics. I get a taste for shootin' and the habit don't break easy. Now shift!'

★ ★ ★

'Yuh listen up good, all of yuh.' Frank Goldman moved slowly across the closed door of the station living-room, paused a moment in the glow of the lantern, the Colt gleaming in the mellowed haze, stared round the faces following him, and halted with his back to the nightblack window. 'I'm for sayin' this once so yuh all understand precisely what Miss Devaux there and m'self expect of yuh, and I shan't be repeatin' it.' He smiled easily. 'Colt'll do the talkin' from here on — where it's necessary. Up to you, ain't it?'

He disregarded Mrs Fitzsimmons' indignant huff and threatening creak where she perched on a spindle-back chair, watched Pepperthwaite adjust his sweat-misted spectacles, and glared into the dark, narrowed gaze of Jim Strange.

'Stage from here to Two Knees Canyon will be under my control,' Goldman went on, flexing the Colt.

'The hell it will!' groaned Spruce from behind the slumped, fevered bulk of Charlie Gills. 'There ain't nobody — '

'I said, my control!' The Colt levelled, its aim clean-cut to Spruce's gut. 'No arguin', not unless yuh want to see the colonel's wife here lose one of them gloved hands she's so fond of flutterin'.'

Mrs Fitzsimmons gulped and seemed unaware of the slow droop of a hat feather. Pepperthwaite's collar tightened visibly. Spruce gritted his teeth across a desperate desire to spit.

'Like I say, my control,' grinned Goldman. 'I'll be ridin' shotgun along of yuh, Mr Wethers, and no arguin' there neither. As for the rest of yuh, Miss Devaux will be callin' the shots. And in case anybody's gettin' the idea that a woman ain't goin' to pose much of a problem, yuh'd best think again. The lady here treads the boards real smart. She shoots a whole sight smarter, and she ain't actin'! Yuh got my word on it.'

Francine Devaux nodded an acknowledgment from the far end of the room, smiled, swirled her skirts and tapped the barrel of her Colt across the palm of her hand.

'I have no idea what you have in mind, or why you are undertaking this ridiculous venture,' said the colonel's wife with a gesture of feigned indifference, 'but, you will not get away with it, of that I can assure you. When my husband gets to hear — '

'Oh, he'll be hearin', lady,' grinned Goldman again. 'Loud and clear, seein' as how he's goin' to be in this right up to his military neck! Sure he is, you right along of him, ma'am.'

'I beg your pardon?' choked Mrs Fitzsimmons, shifting precariously on the spindle chair.

'Shipment of money — real money

— is on its way to Fort Benham right now. Pay-day for the troopers, 'ceptin' they're goin' to have to wait on it. Money ain't goin' no further than Two Knees Canyon.'

'Hell,' croaked Spruce, 'them pay wagons'll be swarmin' with guards. Thick as flies they'll be. Yuh won't get within a spit of 'em.'

'That's true,' sighed Goldman, raising his eyes for a moment to the ceiling. 'Not a hope — not unless yuh got a sure-fire bargainin' hand.' He paused, lowered his gaze, his eyes dancing brightly, and smiled. 'Not unless yuh got the colonel's wife hangin' on her every next breath back of yuh in a stage you're controllin'. Good as money in the bank, ain't it?'

Mrs Fitzsimmons squirmed, tended the miscreant hat feather and stiffened in the grip of her corsets. 'If you imagine for one moment — ' she blurted.

'But I do, ma'am, I surely do. Your husband'll co-operate. Don't have no choice, does he?' Goldman's smile twisted. 'Could take yuh home in pieces, o'course, but I don't figure him for that sorta fellow. Miss Devaux don't, anyhow.'

Mrs Fitzsimmons flashed the actress a chilling glance. Francine Devaux ran a hand down her shapely thigh. Pepperthwaite removed his spectacles and blinked furiously.

'The damned map,' he murmured to himself. 'She had it right there, fastened in her garter.'

'S'right, Mr Pepperthwaite,' drawled Goldman. 'Map detailin' them pay wagons' exact route, times and dates. Miss Devaux's doin'. She can be mighty persuasive when she puts her mind to it. And in case you're wonderin', Mr Wethers, we had our guns stowed in the luggage — Miss Devaux's overnight valise there. Anythin' else you'd like to know?'

'Two of yuh ain't never goin' to pull this off,' growled Spruce.

'That we ain't,' said Goldman, 'which

is why we got some of my boys joinin'
up with us just short of Two Knees.'

'Tell yuh somethin' else, though,'
flustered Hiram Pepperthwaite, still
blinking, 'you ain't reckoned with that
gunslinger sittin' on our tails, have yuh?
He ain't gone away. Still out there some
place.'

'Now there yuh have a real point,
Mr Pepperthwaite,' frowned Goldman,
shifting his gaze to Jim Strange.
'One-time sheriff there brings his own
problems right along of him, don't he?
'Course, there might be a way of dealin'
with 'em, mightn't there? But we'll see,
eh? Chance our arm a mite. Add a
touch of colour to things!'

Strange seemed not to breathe, let
alone blink. Spruce wiped the sweat
from his bristling stubble. Pepperthwaite replaced his spectacles and
turned pale. Mrs Fitzsimmons flashed
Francine Devaux a still more chilling
glance and stiffened her back ramrod
straight.

'And now,' said Goldman, crossing

the room slowly, 'we rest up. Be ready to pull out at first light, Mr Wethers. Fresh team, fast pace.'

'Charlie here's bleedin' to death,' said Spruce. 'He needs a doc.'

'So he's goin' to be unlucky, ain't he?' sneered Goldman. 'He stays here when we leave. No room for extra baggage.'

'Hell,' protested Spruce, 'you do that and you're condemnin' him to death.'

'Precisely,' said Goldman. 'Learnin' fast, ain't yuh?'

12

Sun-up for Sheriff O'Grady trailing the rough mountain track skirting Black Mount to the east came slowly, breaking like a soft blink across the flat night skies before the first dazzling glow lit the morning as if putting a torch to dry brush.

He sat his mount easy as the horse picked its way tiredly between the scatterings of rock, looser drifts of stone and pebble and occasional slivers of sand. He would gladly have traded a half-year's pay for the resolve to slip from the saddle right then and there, find himself some decent shelter and rest his bruised, weary body for just as long as it took for it to seem his own again. But no such luck, not this high into the mountains with a treacherous twenty miles still to go before he caught a glimpse of Charlie Gill's station.

Still, he pondered, coming awake in the sudden chill as night slid away and morning stirred, he had made good progress, uninterrupted, silent and empty, with only the haunting of Cooney Forks to occupy that part of his mind not concentrating on the track.

Lenski would pay for the killing at Cooney, he had grunted to his thoughts, and dearly too — all the way to the worms if he had his way, and Virgil Beattie right along of him. Moran's money would not count for a deal in that reckoning. Even so, the fact that the Beattie boys were on the move so soon was a worry not to be ignored. It stacked the odds still higher against Jim Strange. If Beattie had the nerve to hit the stage — and he was assuming Strange had stayed with it, maybe taking Fishbone's place — then the one-time sheriff of Franckton could start counting out his last hours.

Hell, he had grunted again, Spruce Wethers should have turned the stage around right there at Cooney; at least saved his own and the skins of his passengers. Jim Strange could look to himself. Well, maybe . . .

The light had grown stronger, brighter, the air warmer as it stretched its muscle for the heat to follow, when O'Grady reached the highest point of the track and reined the mount to a halt. Time to take a breather, the pair of them, scan the trail ahead where it began the slow descent to the open plain on the clear run to High Point. Be there well before noon. Time to get himself up-to-date on the stage's progress from Charlie, discover what trail Strange had finally taken, or maybe he had opted for Fort Benham after all.

O'Grady had moved on again, turned on the first sweep of the steadily broadening track, murmured softly to the mount to go easy, pick its own way, when he reined back sharply on the sound of trundling wheels and the slow beat of hoofs.

He shaded his eyes against the glare, peering hard now into the sunlit sprawl far below him. Cloud of dust, swirling like grey breath on the light; outriders, army men, ten, maybe fifteen of them, young-looking officer trailing up ahead; steady pace, no hurry — and then, tight in the circle of riders, two covered wagons, drivers calling encouragement to the teams. Some weight, he thought. Guns and ammunition? Pay money out of Denver? Whatever the cargo, it was warranting a close guard.

O'Grady grunted, relaxed, sat easy, the reins loose in his hands, his gaze softening as the riders and wagons passed slowly, rhythmically on, their trail a straight line through to Two Knees Canyon and Fort Benham. Be there long after the stage, he reckoned.

He rubbed his chin thoughtfully. Maybe he should make himself known. Maybe not. No point at this time in alerting the young officer to a situation he might never cross. Best leave him to his mission.

Even so, he thought, collecting the

reins, useful to know the military were about. Could be an advantage if the Beattie boys got out of hand.

He watched the wagons until the dust cloud was no more than a hazy shimmer and the sounds of wheels and hoofs fading on the thickening morning air. And then he too moved on.

He was thinking of cool water and some restful shade when he turned for High Point.

★　★　★

Mrs Fitzsimmons had determined in her mind that, should the occasion arise — or, more to the point, *when* the occasion presented itself — she would quite cheerfully, albeit carefully, remove her dress gloves and strangle Francine Devaux.

She would take a positive delight in it, she thought, and if, when it was done and there was the time, she would ask — more probably order

— Mr Strange to shoot Goldman. He did not warrant the justice of a fair trial, she had decided.

Meanwhile, there were tactics to be employed in the strategy she had planned through the long hours of that dreadful night. Things to be done before this farcical sitution degenerated into still bloodier chaos.

'I congratulate you, Miss Devaux,' she snorted on the merest flicker of a grin, 'on your gall if not your morals, though I had not appreciated, of course, just how desperate you were. Losing your stage appeal, is that the problem?'

Hiram Pepperthwaite squirmed uncomfortably in the corner and blinked behind his dusty spectacles. Jim Strange opened one eye and focused it on the actress seated opposite him.

'Loss of appeal is a subject you must know a deal about,' smiled Francine Devaux.

'I was just wonderin' here,' began Pepperthwaite hurriedly, 'well, if we might come to some sort of arrangement? I mean, if it comes down to just money.'

'We do not come to arrangements with murderers,' snapped Mrs Fitzsimmons.

'Well, yes, I see the argument in that, but I was thinkin' more along the lines of — '

'Saving your skin, Mr Pepperthwaite?' said the actress. 'I doubt if Goldman would agree to that. He's not the dealing sort in a situation like this.' She shifted the aim of the Colt nestled in her grip. 'And nor am I,' she added flatly. 'But I promise it will be quick. Least I can do for such a devoted follower of my career.'

'And when I think of what I thought I saw in you,' spluttered Pepperthwaite, beginning to sweat, 'it just don't bear — '

'Enough!' snapped Francine Devaux. 'You just hold your tongues, all of you.'

'Lady's right,' said Strange, craning to scan the drift of land beyond the

131

window, 'save yuh breath. Yuh might be needin' all you can get, 'specially if that rider trailin' us far side of the bluff there decides on a closer look.' He swung his gaze to the actress. 'Yuh noticed him, Miss Devaux? Been there since soon after sun-up . . . '

★   ★   ★

'Yuh see him?' croaked Spruce against the whip of wind as he flicked a watery eye to Goldman seated next to him on the driving seat. 'Yuh'd better. He ain't for ridin' on.'

'I see him,' said Goldman, his gaze tight on the rider trailing the distant bluff, hands flexing through his grip on the Winchester. 'He who I think he is — that fella Lenski?'

'That's him, and in case it's crossin' yuh mind, we're way out of range for a shot. No chance of closin' neither, so yuh'd best just stay watchin'.'

Goldman grunted and tapped a finger on the rifle stock.

' 'Course,' Spruce went on with a wry grin to himself, 'that ain't to say the scumbag won't be waitin' on us somewhere in them boulders way out there. Be his best spot for a first shot. Knows we ain't got no options on this trail with an outfit carryin' this weight. Now, if it were me — '

'Yuh always this talkative?' snapped Goldman irritably.

'Nope,' said Spruce, flicking the reins. 'Just takes my mind off that misery we left back there at the station: Charlie Gills roped like a steer to his chair, bleedin' to a slow, painful death. Don't bear thinkin' on. Yuh must have a real warped mind, mister, to leave a fella in that state.'

'Just drive, will yuh?' Goldman spat into the rush of air and growled deep in his throat.

'Somethin' else I been ponderin',' said Spruce as if unaware of the man. 'I been wonderin' just how long it'll be before Moran Beattie catches up with Lenski. Now that could be a whole heap of trouble waitin' on us. Old man Moran ain't much for considerin' things clear through, 'specially when he hears as how he's now lost both his sons and that one-time law-buster, Strange, is still walkin' free. My, is he goin' to be lathered some! Tell yuh straight, mister, you're goin' to have one helluva snappin' mess at yuh heels! I don't reckon for yuh havin' the time to go robbin' no army pay wagons!'

'What say yuh speed things up a mite?' said Goldman, relaxing the rifle in his lap. 'Talk all yuh like, fella, but let's move it, shall we? Fresh team we got here is strainin' on it.'

Spruce snapped the reins and bellowed to the horses. 'You're the boss,' he called. 'But if you're figurin' on us out-runnin' Lenski, we got about as much chance as a spit on the wind.'

And then he too spat and left the spittle to settle where it would.

★ ★ ★

134

'Are we still being followed?' asked Mrs Fitzsimmons, leaning forward to peer at the blurred rush of land through the window.

'Boosted the pace some, ma'am,' said Strange, narrowing his gaze to a squint as he followed the roll of the bluff.

'Is that wise? I'm no authority on stages, but there seems to be an awful lot of this one under some stress.'

'I'm sure Mr Wethers knows what he's about,' ventured Pepperthwaite quietly.

'Oh, yuh can bet to that,' murmured Strange. 'He'll know precisely what he's about.'

Mrs Fitzsimmons leaned back and thudded her hands to her lap. 'Not exactly what you had in mind, is it, Miss Devaux?' she smiled coldly at the actress. 'But, then, real life is not a play, is it? No one knows who's writing the script.' She adjusted the set of her hat. 'And there are so many pitfalls, aren't there? I mean, take that map you have. I suppose you acquired that from my

135

husband? In payment for the dispensation of certain favours, no doubt. On one of his many trips to Denver?'

Francine Devaux smiled softly and levelled the Colt. Pepperthwaite stared, his mouth half open.

Mrs Fitzsimmons examined the seam of a glove. 'Gerald is such an innocent fool on occasions,' she said as if addressing a dinner party. 'Slack as his morals may be, however, his devotion to the military code and practice has never been in doubt — at any time, under any circumstances.' She glanced quickly over the raised gloved hand. 'I would not trust too greatly to your map, Miss Devaux. It might be out of date. Pay shipments are subject to so many variables, you know.'

There had been a moment then when Francine Devaux's grip on the Colt had faltered, eased the merest fraction under the colonel's wife's stare, the condescending flicker of her smile; a moment Strange had spotted, when he tensed and might have made the vital move to grab the woman's arm had the stage not faltered, bounced violently, creaked and groaned as if about to break apart and come to a shuddering halt amid the snorts and whinnying of the horses and Spruce Wethers' tirade of curses.

13

'How bad? And don't give me the big lip version.' Goldman kicked a loose stone into the undercarriage of the stage where it straddled a mound of rocky outcrop like a marooned brown cow on its knees, and glared at Spruce Wethers as if about to break his neck.

Spruce sighed, wiped his sweating face in the folds of a grubby, grease-stained bandanna and slapped the wad of chewing baccy to the side of his mouth. 'Well,' he began slowly, 'hard to say for real 'til I had a close inspection, but right now, from here — '

'I said no lip,' growled Goldman, ranging the probe of his Winchester over Mrs Fitzsimmons, Pepperthwaite and Jim Strange. 'These folk are waitin' on yuh, and so, damnit, am I! Now, how bad?'

'Hit them rocks there at full pace,'

began Spruce again, chewing carefully on the baccy. 'Never saw them under that drift of sand . . . '

Since when had you ever been that blind? thought Strange, lounging at the side of the stage. You know this trail out of High Point for Two Knees Canyon like the back of your hand.

'No, just never saw a darn thing — just kept right on goin'. One eye on that bluff, o'course. Could've been that.'

'So yuh hit the rocks,' snapped Goldman. 'So what's the damage?'

Damn all that could not be put to right good as new in a half-hour, mused Strange, his stare steady on Spruce's face.

'I'd figure for that back axle there takin' the full force. Now, if that's cracked . . . '

Which it certainly is not, smiled Strange to himself.

'Well, could be . . . To be frank, Mr Goldman, we could be lookin' on the prospect of needin' a whole new outfit.'

You are beginning to sound almost convincing, Spruce!

'F'get it,' flared Goldman. 'Yuh get this stage rollin' again and yuh do it now, yuh hear?'

'That's a whole lot easy to say, t'ain't goin' to be nothin' like as simple.'

Goldman probed the rifle menacingly. 'Yuh do it! Now! Otherwise, I get to work here on Mrs Fitzsimmons.'

The colonel's wife stiffened fully upright in a shuddering creak of corset stays. 'You must do as you think fit, Mr Wethers,' she announced. 'Pay no regard to me.'

'Shut it!' growled Goldman. 'Yuh get Pepperthwaite and Strange here to help, and first hint I get of any slackin'.' His stare darkened. 'Just don't call my bluff.'

Spruce shrugged, fastened the bandanna at his neck and spat into his hands. 'Here goes, then,' he said, nodding to Strange. 'Let's get to it, but I ain't makin' no promises.'

'Perhaps I should warn you, I don't

have a none-too-steady backbone,' flustered Pepperthwaite, struggling out of his jacket.

'We noticed!' sneered Goldman.

'Be a man, Mr Pepperthwaite!' chimed Mrs Fitzsimmons. 'Or shall I take your place?'

'That won't be necessary, ma'am,' croaked out Hiram Pepperthwaite. 'I know my duty.'

'Just one thing before we get started,' said Spruce, shading his eyes against the sun's glare as he scanned ahead of him. 'Somebody had better be keepin' a close watch on that bluff out there. Lenski ain't gone away, has he? Two-bits to a dead dog he's watchin' right now.'

* * *

'Gettin' a mite short-sighted in yuh old age, ain't yuh?' hissed Strange into Spruce's ear as they sweated to clear the sand from the undercarriage of the stage.

141

'What do you think?' grunted Spruce, licking the sweat from his lips.

'I think you're a liar — convincin' enough, though, grant yuh that.'

Spruce scooped a mound of sand between his legs. 'Been waitin' on this outcrop for an hour. Hit it sweet as a nut! Couldn't have done it better.'

'So how long we goin' to drag this out?' murmured Strange. 'Goldman ain't exactly the patient type.'

'Long as we can. What yuh reckon? An hour? Mebbe Lenski'll make a move.'

'An hour gives us an edge,' said Strange, rolling aside a boulder. 'Just don't push Goldman to the brink. He's playin' for high stakes and gettin' jumpy with it.'

Pepperthwaite groaned and slid face-down to the sand at Spruce's side.

'Easy there, easy,' soothed Spruce, helping the man back to his knees. 'There ain't no rush.'

'Don't know about that, Mr Wethers,'

coughed Pepperthwaite. 'Way I see it right now — '

'How long?' drawled Goldman, crunching over the sand.

Spruce struggled to his feet, untied the bandanna from his neck and mopped his face. 'Axle crack ain't as bad as it might have been,' he croaked wearily. 'Bad enough, though. Slow us down some. And we got a suspect back wheel that won't be turnin' smoothly. Grease'll help some, but we'll need to stay to the easy trail, 'specially on the approach to Two Knees. Some rough goin' there. Weight too could be a problem, so mebbe we should — '

'I said how long, mister?' clipped Goldman. 'I ain't askin' for a survey.'

'An hour,' said Spruce bluntly. 'But don't hold me to it.'

'I'll do just that!' grinned Goldman, and kicked sand into Pepperthwaite's face.

★ ★ ★

'Do you always place such faith in one man, Miss Devaux?' Mrs Fitzsimmons addressed Francine Devaux without shifting her gaze from the stretch of harsh, sun-baked land to the distant bluff and the lift of clear blue sky topping it. 'I find that quite remarkable.'

The actress stayed silent and made no move, save to steady her grip on the Colt at her side.

'And frankly, my dear,' Mrs Fitzsimmons went on, 'your choice is equally baffling. Mr Goldman there is singularly self-centred. Quite obviously intent on his own ends by whatever the means. Don't you think so?' Her stare shifted like a hawk's at some rustle in the scrub. 'As for Gerald, well, really, he is little more than a poor fool where women are concerned. You must surely know that?' The stare shifted again and hovered. 'Well, perhaps not. But I tell you in all honesty that Gerald is not to be trusted where promises made in the heat of lust are concerned. I should know. You would not be the first I have had to warn.'

Francine Devaux scraped the tip of her boot in the dirt.

'First-class militarily, of course. But, then, you see, everything to Gerald becomes a military operation: assess the potential and strength of the conquest in mind, then bluff, counter bluff, a skirmish here, another there, prod, probe, signal a false intent, risk a minor cost and, presto, you swoop for the kill with the opposition in confusion.' The stare settled unblinking. 'I would hate for you to be deceived — *twice*.'

Francine Devaux had taken a half step forward, hesitated, conscious of Goldman's shadow at her back, when the single shot rang out like the scream of something suddenly trapped, the whine of it climbing on that day's sultry air as if in search of escape.

Francine Devaux swung round in a swirl of skirts and dancing hair. Mrs Fitzsimmons fell back, reaching for a hold on the stage, her hat feathers jostling in a frenzy, mouth opening on a gasp as she watched Goldman stumble, stagger, gather himself in a moan before crashing to the sand, his Winchester pinned beneath him, a trickle of blood oozing in a dark ribbon over the dirt.

Spruce Wethers was the first to scramble from the undercarriage to the actress's side, yell for Mrs Fitzsimmons to 'get yuh butt out of it!' then grab the Colt from Francine Devaux's failing grip.

'Hold the team, Jim,' he bellowed to Strange. 'Don't let 'em spook.'

Pepperthwaite crawled from behind a wheel like a waking insect, his spectacles glinting in the sunlight. 'Is he . . . is he dead?' he groaned, his stare riveted on the sprawled, bleeding mass.

'What he ain't doin' is givin' no more orders!' growled Spruce, stepping through the ribbon of blood to roll the body over with the heave of a worn boot.

⋆ ⋆ ⋆

'Leave him. Let him rot!' Pepperthwaite polished his spectacles vigorously, settled them on his sweat and dirt-streaked nose and squirmed in the sticky cling of his shirt. 'He had no compassion for Mr Gills back there at the station, he ain't deservin' of none now, not in my book.' He ran a hand over his face. 'Pity Lenski's shot didn't finish him.'

'How bad is he?' asked Mrs Fitzsimmons, bending for a closer look at the body cradled in Francine Devaux's lap.

'Bad enough,' murmured Spruce, staring into Goldman's pale, drawn face. 'Lead buried deep. Another whisker to the left and he'd be stiffening. Doubt if he'll live the day.'

'Which is why we should leave him,' said Hiram Pepperthwaite. 'What's the point in lumberin' ourselves with a half-dead body? His plan to take the pay wagon is over, so he probably wouldn't want to live, anyhow. Only a hangin' waitin' on him, ain't there?'

Francine Devaux flashed a searing

glance, Spruce dusted the sand from his stubble. 'Mebbe,' he began.

'No question of it,' huffed Mrs Fitzsimmons, adjusting the perch of her hat. 'We do not sink to Goldman's level, whatever our feelings. He is now a prisoner and will be accorded the appropriate rights. What do you say, Mr Strange? I understand you were once a lawman. What would you do?'

Strange stepped from the shade, stared at the body, caught Francine Devaux's anxious gaze and slung the Winchester to a two-handed grip. 'Wouldn't give the sonofabitch no more room than I would a rat, but you're right, ma'am, we ain't for sinkin' that low.' He narrowed his eyes to scan the shimmering haze of the bluff. 'And we ain't for wastin' time here, neither. No sayin' where Lenski is now or what he's treadin' round that warped mind of his. Could hit us again any time, damn near anywhere he chooses.'

'Tell yuh somethin' else,' said Spruce.

'Don't let's f'get that Goldman's got a whole heap of scum ridin' to join him at the canyon. Ain't nothin' to say they won't go ahead with the pay wagon raid, anyhow. That so, Miss Devaux?'

The actress shrugged. 'This was Goldman's show,' she murmured. 'So who's to say?'

'Let's roll,' grunted Spruce, spitting into his hands. 'Twenty minutes and we'll be movin'. Lend a hand here, Mr Pepperthwaite.'

'Get this trash gunslinger aboard the stage and settle him best we can,' said Strange. 'Yuh handle a Colt, ma'am?' he asked, turning to the colonel's wife.

'After forty years of sharing the same bed with one, I should think so!' grinned Mrs Fitzsimmons. 'You can leave Miss Devaux and her companion to me, Mr Strange. Yourself and Mr Wethers have more than enough to do.'

Say that again, thought Strange, scanning the bluff where soon the shadows would begin to shift and the afternoon light play all manner of tricks.

But Lenski, of course, would know that too.

14

The fist, white-knuckled, fissured in its clench, tight with anger, thudded to the scrub-topped table like a boulder; thudded again, a third time, until the scattered plates, tin mugs, knives and forks and the half-empty bottle of whiskey were shifting and rattling as if in the grip of a rumbling earthquake.

It was a full minute before the silence crept back and the faces of the dozen or so men grouped in the shadowy light of the room ceased to twitch. Only then did Moran Beattie ease himself fully upright and glare like a snake, his black hooded eyes seeming to feast on the fear, and slide his cracked, sun-dried lips to a grin.

'I make myself clear?' he growled, the voice sifting the words like grit. 'You numbskulls capable of understandin' exactly what I'm sayin? Or do I need to shoot some lead and spell it out in blood?'

'Won't be necessary, Mr Beattie, sir,' ventured a tall, loose-limbed wrangler with a twitch in one eye. 'We seen it all. We got it plain enough. Yuh can trust to us.'

Beattie watched the man for a moment, the glare boring deep into his face, the grin hovering, then fading. 'How long yuh been with me, fella?' he asked almost politely.

'Full year now, sir,' twitched the man.

'Full year, eh?' echoed Beattie. 'Twelve whole months, and in that time — summer to summer as I recall — I fed yuh, clothed yuh, provided your roof and your bed and warmth on them cold winter nights and I paid yuh fair. All this I done, eh? Never failed.'

'That's true, Mr Beattie, sir, never failed not once. I ain't complainin'.'

'I bet yuh ain't at that,' sneered Beattie, the voice suddenly colder. 'No good cause to, have yuh, 'cos your world there is complete; cosy as a whore's bed come the snows? Yuh ain't no cause to want.' The fist thudded again. The wrangler shook, his loose limbs slack as rags. 'But I have, damn yuh!' roared Beattie. 'Oh, yes; oh, hell, yes, I have!' He paused, the glare glowing like fire. 'I lost my eldest, Arran, shot down in cold blood back there in Franckton. And yuh all stood witness to that. And now, with him barely gone to bone, what do I find? Yuh all know, don't yuh? Yuh all seen what we found in them hills along the Deadstream trail — my youngest, Virgil, shot through like a dog.' The glare burned across the faces of the men. 'And we all know, don't we, at whose hand? Oh, yes, we know, sure enough: that scumbag, skulkin', renegade lawman, Jim Strange! Him, who should've been taken out my life forever by the so-called fast guns of Pete Lenski and Joe Reisner. Sonsofbitches, pair of 'em!'

Beattie's fist crashed to the table again and swept the mugs and plates to the floor. 'And if that ain't pain and insult enough, I ride in here to the High Point station only to find Charlie Gills bled to death like some hotpokered hog, and this rat' — he swung round to point to the man standing alone at the far end of the room, his stare flat, face expressionless to a squared, tight jaw — 'this fella the misguided folk of Reuben had the misfortune to elect their sheriff, Mr O'Grady no less, makin' himself at home, arrogant as yuh like, still followin' Strange, still lookin' to him. And him, let me remind yuh, bein' the one who smuggled Jim Strange outa town.'

The men waited, silent, watching Beattie's steps between the scattered mugs and plates as if anticipating the next reach of a boot might trigger dynamite.

'So now yuh all see what I want, don't yuh?' growled Beattie again, swinging round. 'I want for us to ride outa here, find that no-good Lenski and finish him right wherever we happen across him — Two Knees Canyon if he's trailin' that stage — and then, and very definitely then, I want Strange, want him real bad, but not dead.' The cracked lips slid back to a grin. 'No, I want him alive, 'cos yuh know why? I'll tell yuh. Strange is goin' to hang, and I want for Mr O'Grady here to have the pleasure of rope-haulin' him every inch of the trail back to Reuben, right to the foot of the hangin' tree at Walt Winnows' livery. That's what I want and that's what yuh goin' to get me!'

'Yuh got it, Mr Beattie, sir,' smiled the wrangler. 'No problem.'

'There'd better not be,' leered Beattie, 'not if yuh all want to stay in them cosy, featherbed jobs yuh got. Now get to it! Bury Charlie Gills decent, look to the mounts, and then we ride. First man falls behind the pace I set is dead!'

The men murmured among themselves and began to disperse under the hawkish gaze of their boss who, when the room had finally emptied, crossed to where O'Grady still stood, silent and staring.

'Yuh heard all that?' said Beattie. 'Made it plain enough, and I ain't foolin' none, O'Grady, yuh mark that.'

'Never doubted it,' drawled out the sheriff. 'Moran Beattie ain't one for spoilin' a good mind, is he? Judge, jury, hangman, he's the whole miserable lot! Free with his henchmen too. I know, I had a visit!'

'Count y'self lucky I didn't say for the boys to finish yuh.'

'Oh, I do,' grinned O'Grady. 'But yuh wrong about Strange. Yuh got no proof he's responsible for what happened here, and yuh wouldn't be lookin' if yuh'd seen the markers on the graves at Cooney Forks. That weren't Strange's doin', not no how.'

'But I do know what happened in Franckton, and I seen Virgil's body with my own eyes. Got it now, out there, side of the corral. Yuh want to see it?'

O'Grady shrugged. 'Don't count for nothin' either way. If Virgil joined up with Lenski on your orders, yuh sent him to his death. Virgil's blood is on your hands, Moran.'

Beattie's eyes hooded to a darkness as if in nightmare, the glint in them no more than pinpricks. 'I could kill yuh for sayin' that,' he croaked.

'So yuh could,' murmured O'Grady, 'and would if yuh could be certain. But yuh ain't, Moran, nothin' like certain. Are yuh? Not that I give a damn right now. I'll just ride with yuh, just like yuh say, 'til you either catch up with Strange, or he finds you. One of yuh's got to be there first. Me, I'm bettin' on it — '

Beattie's fist smashed into O'Grady's face with the force of a rock. 'Damn your eyes!' he cursed, his brow beading sweat.

O'Grady's stare settled again as he fingered the trickle of blood at the corner of his mouth. 'Yuh might live to regret that, Moran. Don't wait if I'm about, will yuh?' He smiled softly. 'Shall we go say a few words over Charlie

Gills? Might be the last chance yuh'll get.'

* * *

Hiram Pepperthwaite had polished every last speck of dirt from his steel-rimmed spectacles, spat on the lens and polished and buffed until they shone clear as pools at the foot of a mountain stream. Never cleaner, never clearer, he thought, as he adjusted them carefully to the bridge of his nose and settled back in the trundling stage to admire and appreciate Francine Devaux in her new role as comforting nurse to the fast fading Goldman.

Got to hand it to her, she had slipped into the part as she might some slinky silk dress. Not a qualm, barely a flicker of distress at the sight of so much blood, the agonized groans in so much pain. Anybody watching might think she really cared.

Not so, of course. No-sir! She was waiting, same as the others, for that last twitch, the breath that would gurgle somewhere back of Goldman's throat before he finally went limp and lifeless. And good riddance to bad scum too, he reckoned. Nobody was going to miss Goldman, Francine Devaux least of all. Question was, what would she do then; what plan had she already hatched deep behind those devouring eyes?

She could give herself up to the law, plead some ridiculous case of being innocently trapped by Goldman into the pay heist plot. But who, in his right mind on the evidence, would believe her? She might try throwing herself on Colonel Fitzsimmons' mercy. But Mrs Fitzsimmons might have something to say about that! This was no territory for thoughts of escape, so . . . well, judging by the look on her face right now and the way she was letting those eyes do all the talking, disregarding almost entirely Mrs Fitzsimmons and the levelled Colt opposite her, she was looking real hard for the next likely body to devour in a feast of charm and enticement and maybe reckoning on having found it.

The heck she had! Hiram J. Pepperthwaite was a man of the world, knew his way around, seen most of the good and bad in folk and could recognize the difference. You bet! He might look an easy catch to anybody's bait, but not so, and especially not to the wiles of a clever actress.

Even so, he had to admit, his spectacles were misting up again. Must be the heat.

★ ★ ★

'Goin' to have to rest the team and water up before we hit the canyon.' Spruce flicked the reins and glanced quickly at Strange riding shotgun. 'Creek just this side of the long bluff. Should be safe enough for what we need. What yuh reckon?'

'Your outfit, Spruce,' called Strange above the beat of hoofs and swish of wheels. 'Do as yuh think best. Can't risk a worn team through Two Knees.

We hit that and we keep goin'.'

'My figurin' exactly.' Spruce flicked the reins again. 'Yuh see anythin' of Lenski?'

'Nothin' yet. He'll be reckonin' he's done enough for now.'

'Surprised he didn't take you out with that shot back there.'

'Not his style,' said Strange, swinging his gaze over the shimmering land. 'He's waitin' on us comin' face to face. And we will, if he waits long enough.'

Spruce grunted and leaned to the pace of the team. 'Question there is, how long *you* goin' to wait?'

Strange stayed silent.

'Goldman's waitin' on only one thing, ain't he? Don't figure for him makin' it to the canyon. Can't say I'll be grievin' for the sonofabitch.' Spruce fell to his own silence for a moment. 'Just what the hell we goin' to do with that actress woman? Hand her over to the military? Could prove a mite embarrassin' for old Colonel Fitzsimmons. Mebbe yuh should pin that badge back on yuh shirt and trail her to stand trial at Reuben. Or mebbe we should . . . Hell, yuh see that, Jim?' he snapped suddenly. 'Up ahead. Tell me I'm seein' things.'

'That you most certainly are not,' said Strange, his gaze narrowed and fixed, hands settling to a new grip on the cradled Winchester as Spruce reined the team to a slower pace on the raised arm of the officer mounted at the head of a waiting group of military a quarter-mile down the sun-hazed trail.

15

'And not one minute before time!' bellowed Mrs Fitzsimmons, gesturing wildly with one hand as she laid her other to the arm of the officer standing to assist her from the stage. 'I have never been so humiliated, not to say insulted *and* assaulted in my life. There are heads to be rolled here, and they will!' She eased gingerly, tiredly to the trail on a waft of stale lavender. 'Nonetheless, I am delighted to see you, Captain Pendrew. How are you?'

'Well enough, ma'am,' clicked the officer, stiffening to attention.

'Glad to hear it,' said Mrs Fitzsimmons, brushing the dirt from an expanse of skirts. 'Wish I could say the same.' She adjusted the hat with an extravagant flourish, poking defiantly at a wayward feather. 'Please be so kind as to see to the dead body we have in there,' she sighed nodding to the shadowed interior of the carriage. 'It's beginning to smell! The young woman cradling it is in my charge.'

'Ma'am?' frowned the captain, peering closer.

'The young woman — Miss Francine Devaux. She is under arrest.'

'But it is Miss Devaux I am here to meet,' said Pendrew, his frown deepening.

'Oh? On whose orders might I ask?' snapped Mrs Fitzsimmons.

'Your husband's, ma'am. Colonel Fitzsimmons. I have explicit orders to meet the stage from Reuben, halt it before it reaches Two Knees Canyon and personally accompany Miss Devaux — ensuring her safety and well-being at all times — to Fort Benham.'

Mrs Fitzsimmons heaved her bosoms to their formidable fullest. 'Really?' she glowered. 'Hardly surprising, perhaps, but I am countermanding them, Captain Pendrew, here and now.'

'But ma'am — '

'But nothing, sir! Forget about your orders.' Mrs Fitzsimmons arranged her gloves importantly. 'I take it my husband made no mention of me? Obviously not. I have returned earlier than expected. And somewhat fortuitously, it seems. That being the case, and in the light of the circumstances — '

'Now just hold up there, will yuh?' said Spruce, raising his arms as he stepped forward. 'Before yuh all get to makin' your private arrangements and settlin' your personal issues, let me just remind yuh this is *my* stage, *my* team — the whole darned shootin' match — and you, all of yuh, are *my* passengers. Ain't nothin' changed on that score since we pulled outa Reuben. And you, Captain whoever-yuh-are, ain't snafflin' one body from under my nose, orders or no orders. And that's fact!'

'I should remind you — ' began the captain, stiffening to his full height.

'You ain't remindin' me of nothin', mister,' dismissed Spruce, slapping a wad of baccy over his gums, 'save mebbe a bad smell, and I ain't referrin' to the dead body we got messin' up the best upholstery. There ain't nothin' in no book saying as how you can take Miss Devaux from this stage. But I can sure as hell tell yuh what you're goin' to do if yuh want to keep them fancy epaulettes gleamin' on your shoulder there: yuh can — '

'I'll handle this, Mr Wethers,' announced Mrs Fitzsimmons.

'We're all goin' to die!' spluttered Pepperthwaite, tumbling from the stage behind his flying spectacles. 'We got a mad gunslinger sittin' on our butts, and if we don't — '

'In hell's name, will yuh all — ' groaned Spruce.

'Captain Pendrew,' smiled Francine Devaux, framing herself in the open stage door space, 'it's been a long time . . . '

It was the throttled curse and

166

warning from Strange that silenced the mayhem of voices and raised a scream in Francine Devaux's throat as a dark, faceless rider raced his mount across the open land towards the stage, his Winchester already blazing.

*   *   *

'Lenski!' groaned Spruce, launching himself at Mrs Fitzsimmons in a floundering mass of chest and paunch and flying limbs as the Winchester lead screeched round him like petrified crows. They hit the dirt with a resounding thud, Spruce's face buried somewhere in the feathers of the woman's hat.

Pepperthwaite scrambled into the shade beneath the stage, his spectacles marooned where they had fallen in the sand, the sweat dripping from his chin in a steady trickle.

Francine Devaux backed into the carriage, fell across the cold, stiffening body of Goldman and screamed again at the touch of congealing blood. She slid to the floor then without another sound and closed her eyes.

Captain Pendrew lost a despairing half-minute, wide-eyed and open-mouthed, before barking the order to 'Take cover!' to his equally bewildered men.

Mounts bucked, pranced, snorted, pawed frantic front legs on tightening reins as the riders fought to stay in their saddles. One man died instantly, shot in the back, clean between the shoulder-blades. Another grabbed his left arm in his right hand on a surge of blood and was thrown into a scramble of rocks where he lay without moving.

Pendrew's sergeant, a barrel-chested, tree-trunk of a man with a tanned, florid face and hawk-dark brown eyes, had rushed to the captain's side in the first hail of fire, only to find himself bucked by the heaving flanks of his own mount and spiralled into a stage wheel hub where the impact pummelled the breath from him in a hissing moan and groan.

The captain's luck in not turning face on from the stage to the line of fire held firm as he dropped to one knee, his Peacemaker Colt already in his grip and roaring.

Only Strange, being the first to see the approaching dust cloud as Lenski kicked his mount to a full, headlong stride, had had the time to fling himself to the dirt and fire at random from his own Winchester. But the target, in the thickening cloud, was vague and blurred, a smudged darkness across the shimmering light, and already heading away from the stage and out of range before he had blinked the sand from his eyes.

'Sonofa-goddamn-bitch! he groaned, his narrowed gaze beginning to water against the settling dust, as he watched Lenski fade on the darker backdrop of a bluff and then vanish beyond it.

Spruce Wethers was the first to stagger to his feet, pushing himself from the mound of Mrs Fitzsimmons like a lizard sliding from a boulder, eyes dancing in his head as he took in the sprawled bodies. 'How in hell . . . ' he began, then, spinning round to gaze piercingly into Pendrew's face, 'and that's only a half of the problems we got!'

The captain could only stare without a sound escaping him.

Pepperthwaite squirmed to the light and blinked on it as if surfacing from the depths of a labyrinth, his face a rubbery mass of sweat.

Francine Devaux crawled away from the dead body, her limbs shivering, lips trembling, hair tossed to a tangled thatch, the bulge of Goldman's stone-cold eyes seeming to follow her in an unblinking gaze.

Jim Strange had come instantly to his feet, crossed to a riderless mount, grabbed the reins and mounted up before Pendrew had scrambled his senses into focus.

'Hold it there, mister,' he snapped.

'That's military property you're handling. Dismount immediately!'

Strange spat the last of the sand from his mouth, wiped a hand across his lips and tipped his hat to bury his face in shadow. 'This ain't no parade ground, Captain, and I ain't no trooper,' he growled. 'Now, appreciatin' yuh ain't had the time to read this situation in full — Mr Wethers'll oblige, I'm sure — but seein' as how yuh already lost two men and your sergeant there ain't lookin' one bit healthy, I don't reckon yuh have much of an argument about me doin' what I should've done long back, which is — go kill a rat-faced scumbag before he gets to boastin' to himself he's goin' to finish the lot of us.' His eyes gleamed from the shadow for a moment. 'Spruce,' he added quietly, 'yuh know what to do, but f'Cris'sake don't trail into Two Knees 'til I'm back. Yuh got it?'

'Got it,' croaked Spruce.

Strange nodded, drew on the reins to

turn the mount and rode out towards the bluff.

'Don't say a word, Mr Pendrew,' ordered the colonel's wife, wincing to the creak of her corsets as she smoothed the feathers of her hat into shape, 'or you'll have me to answer to!'

'Just what in the name of sanity is happenin' here?' flustered Pepperthwaite, blinking for his vision through the cracked lenses of his spectacles.

'Nothin' that a little grave-diggin' hereabouts won't put from your mind, Mr Pepperthwaite,' said Spruce, spitting the wad of baccy to the dirt. 'What say we clean up, eh?'

16

O'Grady's day was fast beginning to leave a bad taste in an already parched mouth. Events since his last sight of the military wagons trundling their slow way to Fort Benham, his descent from the hills to the misery he had found at High Point, and the arrival at the station to take him completely by surprise of Moran Beattie and his boys, had snared his thinking and left him with a cold chill in the pit of his stomach. And not least, a whole stampeding herd of questions.

No doubt that Jim Strange had taken out Virgil Beattie, but where now was Lenski? Where was the stage? Was Strange still with it? What had happened at High Point; whose hand to the tortured death of Charlie? What precisely did Moran have in mind, where, when, and how? And just what in hell was he going to do about it?

Plan on some escape? He might, he had figured, have stood some chance if Beattie had held to the trail directly west. That route would have brought them to the tails of the army wagons and an encounter that would have been a gifted diversion for escape.

No such luck. Beattie had opted for the rougher but faster trail northwards to reach Two Knees Canyon.

Stand to a face-to-face showdown with Beattie? Sure, and he might pull it off, save for the dozen or so guns waiting at his back.

Keep going, take his chances wherever they occurred, hope that he might slip clear to stand to Strange once they found him? Did he have a choice? No choice, he had decided, five miles out of High Point. Beattie's eyes were forever on him, watching his every move, almost waiting for the one that would give Moran just the excuse he needed to draw on that long-barrelled Colt tucked at his side.

It was coming, anyway, mused O'Grady. Whatever Beattie's plan, there would be no place come the close of it for witnesses of doubtful loyalty, who were not on Moran's payroll, who were not for his twisted hatred of Jim Strange and, more certainly, just happened to be wearing a law badge.

Count the hours, O'Grady, he had thought, they are all named and numbered . . .

Day rolled endlessly, pitilessly to dusk and nightfall with Beattie still setting the pace northwards; no resting up, respite, save only to state the thirsts of weary mounts; nothing asked, nothing said; every man for himself and most too scared to fall a yard behind the hell-for-leather man out front and the bouncing bundle of death strapped tight to the trail mount back of him. As in life, Virgil Beattie, was going the hard way to his resting place.

O'Grady was reckoning on Two Knees being the destination Beattie had settled on — figuring he would be there well ahead of the stage — when, as the pace slowed for the descent from high country to the sprawl of a tight-necked gully, Moran raised an arm for the riders to halt. 'And not a sound out of any one of yuh,' he growled, wiping the dirt-pitted sweat from his face as he peered into the depths of the shadowed gully.

It was a long, near silent minute, broken only by the snorts of mounts, the soft jangle of tack, crease of leather, wheezing of tired men, before Beattie gestured for O'Grady to ease up alongside him.

'You know about this?' he grunted, nodding to the trail below.

O'Grady leaned forward, his hands soft on the reins, eyes narrowed to tight, watchful slits. 'Eight riders,' he murmured quietly. 'Trailed from the north for some days, I'd reckon. Goin' easy, real quiet. Ain't for bein' heard or noticed.' He paused, the gaze deepening. 'Provisioned up, judgin' by them followin' packs. And carryin' an awful lot of iron there for common drifters.'

'They ain't no drifters, mister,' drawled Beattie, wiping a hand across his mouth. 'More like scumbag raiders, rustlin' types, 'ceptin' there ain't a head of beast these parts worth the botherin' to. Packin' enough guns 'tween 'em to start a war.' He spat across a boulder. 'So what yuh figure?'

What was there to figure, wondered O'Grady, frowning as he peered again? Eight full-armed and provisioned men, tough, rough-looking who might be about just anything wrong side of the law, but in no way drifting. No, these fellows had a destination and were intent enough on it.

'Well?' asked Beattie.

'Nothin' — nothin' I heard speak of and I ain't seen none of 'em before. Suggest we don't tangle, though. They look mean enough to be left well alone.'

Beattie grunted and spat again. 'Where they headin'?'

Now that, thought O'Grady, he would give a month's pay to know.

But wait, figure it: tracking from the north; could be they had come on the long trail out of Denver, slipped away unheard, unseen through bleak, barren country; moving steadily south. To where? Nothing here of note until you swung east for Reuben, and sure as hell nothing in Reuben for men the likes of these types, all set to shake the dirt of dead lands from their boots. So . . . Two Knees Canyon coming up if, at the mouth of the gully, they turned west. But would they? What would eight roughneck gunslingers, ironed up to the teeth, want with a place like Two Knees?

It was then that O'Grady swallowed and barely noticed the sour taste in his mouth; then that his eyes began to widen, soaking in the light as if seeing it for the first time; then that his fingers tapped lightly over the loose reins and he was back again on that lone trail out of the hills heading for High Point and watching the slow progress of heavily guarded, laden wagons; then that he began to wonder if he was thinking the wildly impossible, but staying sane enough to believe it.

'To be frank, I wouldn't have a clue where they're headin',' he murmured.

* * *

A mountain lion would wait all day on the scent of its prey and kill with ease when the light grew thin. Strange had nothing like all day, not even an hour of it, but Lenski had all the time he needed and some to spare if the fancy took him.

The thought raised a prickling sweat in Strange's neck long before he reached the shadowed sprawl of the bluff, rode swiftly but deeply into the straggle of dead brush and rock cover, dismounted and waited in the shade with only a high, drifting hawk for company.

No saying where Lenski had gone to ground since swinging away from the shooting, but you could bet every yard of it would be of his choosing. All very neat, thought Strange, blinking on the shimmering haze beyond the shade, no less than he would expect of an all-time gunslinger whose very existence lay in the balance of a gun to the hand, the instinctive sense of when to fire, when to ease back, when to be a target, when to fade to a shadow of it.

Lenski's seemingly hare-brained, single-handed attack on the stage had been carefully calculated: wait for Strange, Spruce Wethers and the passengers to be fully occupied in their meeting with the military, then swoop, take out whoever happened to be in the line of fire, race clear and wait for Strange to make his move.

Bag of gold to a marked deck he would follow. They always did in Lenski's book. Nothing so certain as a riled man to take the bait for seeking revenge.

Strange blinked again, settled his grip on the Winchester and scanned the ground above and beyond him.

Nothing to be gained yet in climbing higher — too obvious too soon — so safer to move forwards, hugging the shade, staying tight in the boulders and rocks. Lenski would have seen him ride out from the stage, watched him disappear into shade, reckoned on how long he would wait, pondered his options and probably be smiling to himself right now on the predictability of it all.

Seen it before, any one of a dozen places, dozen fellows all doing exactly the same. Almost too damned easy, when you came to think it through.

Strange shifted quickly, bent low, footfalls firm over the looser rocks, gripping for balance in the reaches of slack sand. Air was thicker, heavier here, so that he was forced to pause to steady his breathing at every few yards. Time then for another quick scan, to wait, listening now for the slightest sound, the merest hint of another presence.

But not yet, not this close, he

thought. No, Lenski would want to lure him on, bring him to the ground of his choice where the odds would only ever be stacked one way.

He moved on, aware now of the land beginning to lift on a slow, straggling slope to the high cheek of the bluff. Steady up here, he thought. If Lenski was somewhere up there — where else, damn it? — he would have a view that would miss nothing in whichever direction it swept.

Pause. Listen. Wait for the sweat to settle. Ease the grip on the rifle. Tighten it. Move again.

Steeper now, more difficult to find a foothold. Would only take the crash of a larger rock for Lenski to have a target he could hardly miss. Another step, another climb higher. Firmer ground shelving gently to the cover of a bulging boulder. Time to rest up, cool off in the shade, catch the breath, figure on precisely where . . .

Strange's thoughts melted to slide cold as ice water at the back of his head at the sudden slithering movement at his feet.

Rattler!

'In hell's name,' he groaned, backing deeper to the boulder as the shape glided like a shaft of darkness across his boots. He froze, tightened until it seemed his limbs were roped, the sweat beading in a surge across his eyes, trickling down his cheeks, dripping from his chin. The snake had halted, the tail twitching angrily, head lifting to focus its bewitching stare into Strange's eyes.

'Easy there, easy,' he moaned, fingers aching in their grip on the rifle as the rattler continued to stare, sway slightly, flash the flame of tongue, begin to rattle as if rehearsing the ritual movements of a death dance.

Strange's concentration on the rattler, his gaze riveted to the snake's stare as if the mesmeric glare of it were drawing his eyes from their very sockets, had broken his attention on the movement around him. He saw nothing of the growing shadow above him, nothing of its slow glide from behind the boulder to pass like a fleeting cloud over the slope; heard nothing of the step that murmured across the dirt somewhere behind it, the click of a Colt hammer lost in the menacing rattle.

Not until a boot scuffed dirt and the shadow settled did he flick his gaze from the snake to stare into the grinning slant of Lenski's lips, the gleam of triumph in his pale-blue eyes, the glinting prod of the gun barrel levelled straight and steady in the gunslinger's grip.

'Well, now,' tittered Lenski, his eyes widening, lips breaking to an almost boyish smile, 'ain't this just somethin'? What'll I do, Strange, shoot yuh through, put yuh outa your misery, or leave yuh to the rattler? Decent fella'd shoot the rattler, o'course, but I ain't got a spark of decency in me where you're concerned! 'Course I could blow the rattler's head to mush and give yuh a half chance — be a whole sight more satisfyin' to see you outgunned — but, well, I don't know . . . what yuh fancy?'

Strange swallowed, blinked on a surge of sweat, tightened his grip on the Winchester and watched the rattler. 'Hard to tell from here just who *is* the snake!' he croaked. 'Ain't nothin' separatin' yuh.'

Lenski flinched. The grin slid away. 'Doin' this for Joe as much as anyone, yuh know that, don't yuh?' he drawled. 'Couldn't give a spit for yuh m'self, but seein' as how Moran Beattie and his boy'll be headin' this way soon, and reckonin' on him being real sore about losin' both his kin to your ready gun, I figure for him bein' more than happy for me to bring yuh body in. Goin' to make his day, ain't it?'

'Wouldn't set a deal of store to pickin' up the money, though,' grated Strange, his gaze still tight on the rattler. 'Beattie might just be thinkin' yuh fouled up where Virgil was concerned. Yuh did too. Should never have left him to stand alone.'

'But he ain't never goin' to know that, is he?' leered Lenski. 'Not once I shut your mouth for good.'

The snake hissed again, glared, flashed its tongue and rattled viciously.

'Gettin' impatient, ain't he?' mouthed Lenski, freshening his grip on the Colt. 'So am I! Time I was all through with yuh. Get to renewin' my interest with them stage folk back there, 'specially that good-lookin' woman. She's somethin' else.' He flexed the Colt again, the light glinting across its smoothness. 'Yuh ready?'

Strange tensed. There was going to be just one chance for what had spun like a whirlwind into the jumble of his mind. A fifty-fifty bid, no stretching the odds. He glanced quickly at Lenski, then at the snake, this time returning the glare without flinching, the cold look of fear, his lips grimacing to a tight line, and in one lightning swish of the rifle lifted the snake from in its sway and tossed it like a length of torn twisted ribbon at Lenski.

The gunslinger's snarl ahead of the blaze of his Colt bared his teeth and narrowed his eyes, but the shot was high and wild as the rattler spun across his chest and buried itself in a twisted, clinging coil round his neck. Lenski's eyes rolled to wide, white balls. He snarled again, dropped the Colt and scrambled his fingers over the writhing body, falling back now under the shuffling, scuffing swish of his boots through loose rocks and dirt.

Strange's Winchester roared in a volley of fire from the hip, ripping into Lenski's gut and chest, but he was already dead, sprawled halfway down the slope between a bulge of boulders long before the echo had faded and the rattler slithered away to the silence of shade.

The bite marks in Lenski's neck were plain enough to see; his shirt a soaked mass of blood. 'Got the venom of both worlds there, didn't yuh?' murmured Strange as he strolled away to the foot of the bluff.

17

'Yuh hear that, Mr Wethers? Gunfire. Colt followed by a Winchester. I rather think Mr Strange is all through out there. Would you not agree, Captain Pendrew?'

Mrs Fitzsimmons heaved her bosoms into place as if about to sweep into a civic reception.

'I agree, ma'am,' said Pendrew, turning to peer into the shimmering haze at the bluff. 'Colt then rifle fire, but that is not to say — '

'Perhaps we should make a move, Mr Wethers,' boomed the colonel's wife dismissing the officer. 'The day wears on and I fancy you will not welcome the prospect of the canyon at dusk.'

'Nossir, ma'am,' croaked Spruce, rubbing his chin as he rolled the chewing baccy noisily, 'I want clear of Two Knees soon as possible, but like I been tellin' the captain here, we got a whole heap to consider.'

'Not least your passengers, of which I am still one,' sniped Pepperthwaite from the shaded side of the stage.

'I ain't one bit unaware of my passengers,' snapped Spruce, 'but I ain't for throwin' yuh to the dogs unnecessarily neither.'

'The first priority is to ensure that we do not find ourselves in the crossfire of the hordes of gunslingers we seem to have about to descend on us,' said Pendrew, slapping his hands together behind his back as he began to pace. 'There's been enough killing if what you tell me is fact, Mr Wethers. Time to call a halt. I suggest, therefore, that I have two of my remaining men here ride out to join the approaching pay wagon from Denver and bring it to a halt until we are able to call up reinforcements from Fort Benham. I could spare another man to reach Colonel Fitzsimmons with a message of our plight. That done, we must then reach the comparative cover of Two Knees and hole-up until help arrives.' He halted mid-stride and stared at the bluff again. 'Mr Strange is doubtless able to more than look to himself. We, meanwhile — '

'You assumin' command here or somethin', mister?' frowned Spruce, still rolling the baccy.

'Somebody has to,' glared Pendrew. 'You have done your best, Mr Wethers, and I am sure your efforts will not go unrewarded, but these matters have now taken on an entirely different perspective.'

Spruce shot a fount of spittle to the dirt. 'You bet they have, mister! And I'm tellin' yuh square up, we ain't — '

'You should perhaps take a look at the new perspective riding in,' interrupted Mrs Fitzsimmons as she pointed to the steadily approaching cloud of dust on the northern horizon. 'I fancy we are about to have company.'

Spruce and the captain shielded their eyes against the glare as they scanned the growing smudge of grey dirt cloud and the vague darker images at the heart of it.

'Riders — whole handful of 'em,' muttered Spruce darkly. 'Hell, they could just be . . . ' He swung round to Francine Devaux where she lounged alone in the shade. 'Them who I think they are, lady?' he croaked.

'Very likely, Mr Wethers,' smiled the actress, drumming her long soft fingers on the rim of the stage wheel. 'And right on time.'

'Sonofa-goddamn-bitch,' sighed Pepperthwaite, pushing his spectacles into the bridge of his nose. 'Them's Goldman's men,' he mouthed. 'Just like he said. Hell, we're way outnumbered. It'll be a bloodbath!'

'Hold up there,' barked Pendrew, gesturing to his ragged, dust-caked band of men. 'Corporal Trotter, bring the men into line, arms at the ready, but not, I repeat not, a single shot to be fired. We have too much at stake here. Mr Wethers, I suggest you get — '

'I know, I know!' groaned Spruce. 'Don't have to tell me, f'Cris'sake. Ain't a hope of outrunnin' the scum. So . . . Mrs Fitzsimmons, Mr Pepperthwaite, yuh take cover in the stage, both of yuh, and no showin' y'selves.' He glared at Francine Devaux. 'Yuh know these fellas?'

'In passing.' The actress gazed at the gathering dust cloud. 'Hardly my types, but I think you will find their leader to be one by the name of Daggs. Not a pleasant man.'

'And you, my dear, would surely know,' huffed Mrs Fitzsimmons, climbing aboard the stage. 'No compromising, Mr Pendrew,' she barked. 'We are all for survival, but not for bargaining with vermin robbers.'

'Yuh speak for y'self, ma'am,' muttered Hiram Pepperthwaite. 'Any of us come out of this alive, it'll be a miracle.'

'Oh, do stop whining!' The colonel's wife settled herself with a thud. 'Any sign of Mr Strange yet?'

'Not a hair of him, ma'am,' said

Spruce, closing the stage door.

Mrs Fitzsimmons leaned forward, a hat feather drooping sadly across her brow. 'Good,' she murmured with a wink and a wry smile. 'That gives me all the hope I need.'

★ ★ ★

He was tall, well-set, with a slow, easy shift of his limbs that gave a false impression of being casual, until you caught the fiery sharpness in his eyes. A man on a short fuse, thought Spruce, watching Daggs pace carefully through the shade, his men — eight of the mangiest drifters he could imagine — mounted silently in line at the back of him. A man of scant patience and doubtless an instinctive twitch to lay his grubby hands to the holstered twin Colts at his hips at the slightest provocation. You would not choose to tangle with the likes of Daggs, mused Spruce, not if you had a fancy for staying alive. He would kill just for the sheer hell of it.

'Shame,' he was saying, his gaze following the measured pace of his steps. 'Me and Goldman went back some. Colorado, California . . . Met up again back there in Denver. Still, that ain't for mournin' over, is it?' His gaze lifted like a widow's black veil. 'No, no, we got other matters — and we still got the colonel's wife there, ain't we? Still got the bargainin' pawn. Good. I like that. So . . .'

Daggs paced on to stand at the back of Francine Devaux. 'Yeah . . . ' he mouthed, his hands settling on the actress's shoulders. 'So we get to this just like Goldman planned.'

'Over my dead body!' croaked Pendrew.

'Very likely, mister,' leered Daggs, his gaze flicking angrily to the captain. ''Course,' he went on, 'I got the burden of these military scum, ain't I? Could kill yuh now, Captain. Get it over with. What yuh say?'

Pendrew stiffened and sweated. 'Suit

yourself, of course, but I can assure you — '

'No, yuh can't,' snapped Daggs. 'There ain't nothin' yuh can stand assured of, save eatin' dirt minute I decide on it. So yuh shut it, mister. Tight!' He glanced over the line of troopers. 'Before we get to killin' yuh, though, yuh single out one of these men to ride to Fort Benham with a message for Colonel Fitzsimmons.'

'The hell I will!' flared Pendrew.

'Yuh right, mister, the hell you surely will!' Daggs lifted a hand to his men. 'Get down here, Blades, and go drag that colonel's woman outa the stage.'

A one-eyed heap of a ragbag fellow slid from his mount and tittered childishly as he crossed to the stage, opened the door, and reached for the bulk of Mrs Fitzsimmons.

'Hands off, rat!' barked the colonel's wife, cracking a fist across the man's hand. 'If my presence is required, I am perfectly capable of making my own entrance.'

And she was too, thought Spruce, stifling a soft grin on a new wad of chewing baccy, as he watched Mrs Fitzsimmons loom like a vast black shroud in the stage door, her corset stays creaking menacingly, the hat perched tight and firm on her head.

'And just who the devil are you?' she snarled at Daggs, brushing Blade's clawing hand aside with a swoop of her own. 'And get this infested piece of rubbish out of my sight!'

'No messin', lady,' quipped Daggs. 'This ain't Fort Benham and I ain't the stomach for middle-aged dramatics. Now, you just get down and here. Blades, I wanna feather from that bonnet and a chunk of the old witch's hair. Do it!'

Spruce winced and screwed his eyes at the sight of Blades' approach with a knife drawn and glinting on the sunlight in his hand.

'No need for such antics, my man,' boomed Mrs Fitzsimmons, turning viciously on Blades as she removed the hat, pulled a handful of feathers from its thatch and without a qualm or murmur of pain drew strands of her hair from the back of her head in one decisive tug. 'Primitive,' she announced, handing the samples to Daggs. 'I suppose these are to be sent on to my husband with a message to say that the rest will follow in blood-soaked pieces unless he has the good sense not to scupper your plans to raid the pay wagons? Primitive! Meanwhile, I remain hostage. So be it.' She settled the hat again and thrust her bosoms to their limits. 'You will comply, Captain Pendrew, no arguing.'

'But, ma'am — ' protested Pendrew.

'No buts, there is not the time. Just do whatever is required and let's get on with it.'

'Why, thank yuh, ma'am,' grinned Daggs sardonically. 'That's real co-operative.'

'I'll still have you flogged, whoever you are,' glared the colonel's wife, stepping back to the stage door in a swirl of skirts. 'You too!' she snarled at Blades. 'Before you hang, that is!' She turned to Spruce. 'A hand to assist me, if you please, Mr Wethers. I fancy our new-found companions are anxious to be moving.'

Spruce came to Mrs Fitzsimmons' side, took her hand and balanced her back to her seat. 'Thank you,' she smiled, then, leaning close again, whispered, 'The bluff, Mr Wethers. Take a look. I fancy Mr Strange is moving.'

18

The bad taste in O'Grady's mouth had worsened; there was not a muscle in his body that was not still protesting the beating he had taken back at Reuben, and now, in the heat of a stifling day, with the buzz of flies, beat of hoofs and ceaseless jangling of tack and creaking of dry leather pounding through his head, he was all for taking a wild chance and breaking clear of Beattie and his marauding mob at the next twist on the mountain trail.

Or had he left it far too late, he wondered, slowing at Beattie's side as the track twisted between the sprawl of high boulders?

Too late to turn and ride back to the army wagons still trundling the main trail to Two Knees Canyon, that was for sure. A whole sight too late to investigate the gunfire they had heard along the roll of the distant bluff. Too late to take a closer look at the ironed-up drifters, and maybe far too risky. And too late by a long stride to ponder the fate of the stage and Jim Strange. He was going to find out soon enough.

'I ain't for nosyin' into them,' Beattie had announced once the drifters had passed. 'Let 'em go. They ain't our concern.'

Wrong, O'Grady thought, but stayed silent.

'My reckonin' is that Strange and the stage are headin' fast for Two Knees,' Beattie had continued. 'And so, I fancy, are we.'

'And Lenski?' O'Grady had asked quietly. 'What yuh figure for him? Been a deal of gunfire hereabouts. Mebbe we should go take a look.'

'No time for pokin' about, mister. We ride for Two Knees. That's where we're goin' to settle all this, one way or the other.'

O'Grady could see one way clear

enough, but he doubted if Beattie had the remotest idea of where the 'other' might be leading, or what he might find at the Canyon.

And why take the trouble to warn him, he reflected, swinging to another twist as the trail grew steeper? An hour's ride and he would see for himself. Meantime, only thing to do was swallow on the sourness in his mouth.

It was beginning to taste like poison.

★ ★ ★

'Well, now, Miss Devaux,' smiled Mrs Fitzsimmons, supporting her bulk against the sway of the stage, 'I suppose you consider the tables turned, as they say? You have the edge, is the phrase they use. Is that not so?'

'Too right,' said the actress, nestling the butt of a Colt in her grip. 'Like you say, the edge — sharp as a blade.'

Hiram Pepperthwaite shifted uncomfortably. 'Can't think how yuh ever got involved with a type like Daggs,' he murmured, looking away.

'Depends what you mean by involved.'

'I think we all know what Mr Pepperthwaite means,' sniffed the colonel's wife. 'I can't imagine a man like Daggs being content with mere money when there's a woman such as yourself on offer. You take my meaning?'

Francine Devaux's glare hardened. 'He can try,' she grinned. 'That's about all he will do.'

Mrs Fitzsimmons steadied herself again. 'I doubt it. Surely, with Goldman out of the way he sees you as a bonus in this ridiculous escapade. Mark my word on it, my dear, he has plans for you. Most unsavoury, I should say, from a man who appears not to have washed in weeks!'

Pepperthwaite adjusted his spectacles. 'T'ain't too late, miss. I mean, yuh could still come out of this and no real harm done. Way I figure it, all yuh'd need to do — '

'We are not for bargaining, Mr Pepperthwaite,' snapped Mrs Fitzsimmons. 'Miss Devaux has made her bed — one of many, I don't doubt — and she must lie on it. Rest assured, we shall survive. We have the law.'

'Well, I ain't catchin' no sight of it,' groaned Pepperthwaite, staring into the empty, sunlit land. 'I'd sure as hell like to know how yuh figure for us seein' another sun-up. Might not even make sundown, damnit!'

'I'll ask Daggs to make it fast for you,' grinned the actress.

'I wouldn't,' huffed Mrs Fitzsimmons, stiffening sharply. 'He's almost certain to demand payment in kind for the slightest favour. You could find yourself physically bankrupt in days!'

The stage lurched and groaned to a rough stretch of trail drowning Francine Devaux's snarled retort as her grip on the Colt whitened her knuckles.

★　★　★

Spruce Wethers flexed his grip on the reins to steady the team, glanced quickly at Daggs seated next to him, then turned his gaze slowly to catch what he could of the trail they had just cleared beyond the squad of Daggs's men surrounding the troopers and Captain Pendrew.

Mrs Fitzsimmons had been right: Strange had been there at the bluff, no more than a blurred smudge among the first lift of rocks and boulders, but there, in one whole piece, mounted up and watching. The showdown with Lenski had gone his way, but now what? He would have figured the new arrivals at the stage being Goldman's men — figured too that his only choice was to stay clear of them and out of sight — so would he follow at a distance, get ahead of the stage on the longer trail to Two Knees to the east, make a run for Fort Benham, wait for the army wagons to catch up, or had he maybe got a sight of Moran Beattie and his men?

Hell, thought Spruce, the options crowded in thicker than a dust storm which reminded him, he grunted to himself, turning his gaze back to the trail ahead, there was a heap of bad weather coming in from the west. Air had thickened some, breeze dropped to little more than a babe's breath, and the cloud began to build thick and black out of Benham to sit like a hunched old man over the canyon.

'Yuh see that?' he called to Daggs. 'Foul weather dead ahead. We'll hit it under the hour.'

'Don't fuss me none,' mouthed Daggs, peering ahead. 'What's with yuh? Yuh don't like the rain? Cool things down a bit.'

'Rain? I ain't talking *rain*, mister,' shouted Spruce against a sudden screech of protesting wheels. 'I'm talking storm — dirt, dust, sand; wind like yuh ain't never felt before, 'specially up there in Denver. Tell yuh something, fella, wind like we could be headin' for could turn this stage to matchwood. I know, I seen it. Took a whole wagon train out five years back. Yuh hear about that in Denver?'

'No, can't say I did,' drawled Daggs wearily.

You bet you never did, smiled Spruce to himself, with a flick of the reins, because no wagonmaster worth a spit would ever trail a train through Two Knees!

'Wind took a dozen wagons clean outa sight. Never did see them again.' Spruce smacked his gums and spat over a limb of rock. 'Rags, few bones, timbers, one wheel . . . not a body seen again. Old Fury had the lot of 'em.'

'Old Fury?' frowned Daggs. 'What the hell yuh talkin' about?'

'Old Fury — name they give that canyon wind when the storm blows up. Whips clean through them rocks like the breath of Hell itself.'

'Will yuh just get to the driving, f'Cris'sake?' growled Daggs.

'Sure,' called Spruce, snapping at the reins. 'Do the best I can — *while* I can.'

It was a long, silent minute before Daggs spoke again, his gaze narrowed beneath a furrowing frown on the distant stormcloud. 'How bad's that weather goin'to be?' he croaked, without looking at Spruce.

'Bad enough, I'd reckon,' sighed Spruce, as if resigned to the inevitable. 'Goin' to hold yuh up some, and them army wagons when they hit this trail.'

Another half-minute of silence with Daggs still concentrated on the cloud. 'What yuh suggest?' he asked reluctantly.

'Me? You are askin' *me* when you're sittin' there with a handful of aces? Mister, you're callin' the shots here.'

'I'm askin' yuh!' snapped Daggs. 'Just tell me, will yuh?'

Spruce cracked the reins, spat and leaned forward knowingly. 'Well . . . ' he drawled slowly, 'I'd figure for it bein' safest to pull in deep on the leeside. There's a long, high overhand. Best protection there is — *only* protection, come to that. We hole-up there a whiles 'til the worst of the blow is through, we might, just might, make it. Never no sayin' for certain, o'course. I seen the time — '

'Yeah, yeah, I'm sure yuh have,' clipped Daggs. 'We'll do it, soon as yuh think fit.'

'Yuh got it, mister!' called Spruce, stifling a mocking grin. 'Two Knees, here we come, Hell and all!'

Blow, wind, blow, he prayed, cracking the reins again.

⋆　⋆　⋆

'I sense a change in the weather, Mr Pepperthwaite,' said Mrs Fitzsimmons, wafting the frills of a lace handkerchief at her cheeks. 'Storm brewing,' she announced definitively.

'I agree,' nodded Pepperthwaite, averting his gaze from Francine Devaux's moon-eyed stare. 'Temperature's been climbin' for an hour. First thunder in a few minutes.'

'Typical of the territory, Mr Pepperth-waite. The colonel always maintains — '

'Will you two just cut the cackling?' flared the actress.

'My, my,' simmered Mrs Fitzsim-mons, 'getting a shade jumpy, aren't we, Miss Devaux? Surely a mere storm hardly bothers a person of your nerve?'

'Some folk get to bein' real spooked come a storm,' offered Pepperthwaite, pushing at his spectacles. 'My old Aunt Jemima took to rootin' right under the homestead out Montana way. Couldn't stand a crack of thunder, and, hell, the wind — '

'Ah, the wind, Mr Pepperthwaite. Yes, indeed the wind,' said the colonel's wife, wafting the handkerchief to a lacy flurry. 'Now that, in these parts, especially through Two Knees Canyon, is quite frightening.'

'Enough! I am not interested,' snapped the actress.

'No, Miss Devaux,' said Mrs Fitzsim-mons craning forward to stare directly into the moon-eyes, 'you may not be, but there are others out there who very well might.'

The stare was still fixed and tight when the sun went in and the wind began to howl.

19

Jim Strange lowered his head to the sudden whip of the wind, blinked against a flying surge of sand and headed his mount into the cover of the rocks closest to hand.

'Easy there, easy,' he murmured to the mare as she snorted and pawed nervously at a surface that had begun to slither and slide like a disturbed nest of snakes. He lowered and tightened the brim of his hat, pulled his still sweat-soaked bandanna over his nose and eyes, patted the mount's neck and swung his narrowed gaze over the already smudged shapes and outlines in the gloom of the gathering storm.

Somewhere in the teeth of the wind and far ahead of him, the grind and creak of the stage, the jangle of tack on shortening reins faded to an echo. Spruce would be making a run for it, he thought, driving the outfit deep into the shelter of the canyon. Simply a matter of sitting it out then, waiting on the arrival of the army wagons. But how long, he wondered, before Goldman's band of raiders got restive? How long before Captain Pendrew's instinct to make a move got the edge on his better judgement? How long before the storm blew itself out? Would the lone rider he had seen split from the company and head out for Fort Benham make it?

Strange grunted and murmured softly to the mare as the wind whipped and another surge of sand, dirt and loose scrub spiralled on the gust.

Sitting it out might suit the raiders — Spruce Wethers and his passengers had no choice — but that was no good reason for him to join them. Time had come to make his own move, put the cover of the storm to the only advantage that seemed feasible: trail back to the army wagons, find and halt them and leave the raiders to fathom their own tactics.

Easy to figure, not so easy to get to, he thought, swinging the mount round. Only advantage being he would have the wind at his back. But was that the only thing? There had been no sight as yet of Moran Beattie and his men. So just where were they holing-up — if they were?

* * *

'Goddamnit, if I don't sometimes get to wonderin' if the good Lord Himself ain't snappin' at my backside!' cursed Beattie, pulling the collar of his shirt high into his neck before licking the sand and sweat from his lips and spitting viciously.

And He probably is too, thought O'Grady, rolling his bruised shoulders against the buffeting gusts. 'Yuh goin' to sit this out or keep movin'?' he shouted through the howl, his eyes narrowed to the tightest slits. 'That stage'll be holed-up in Two Knees by now; yuh ain't seen hide nor hair of

Strange, and I wouldn't trust to them drifters bein' all peace and light neither. And what about them gunshots?' O'Grady wiped a hand across his mouth. 'This ain't goin' one bit to plan, Moran, so what yuh goin' to do?'

Beattie spat again, pulled at his hat and eyed the smudge of his huddled men. 'Don't figure for nobody goin' no place, not 'til this is done,' he called. 'We'd best sit it out.'

'You're beginnin' to sound like a man waitin' on somethin' turnin' up,' mocked O'Grady. 'T'ain't your style, Moran. Yuh surprise me.'

'Stay surprised, O'Grady,' growled Beattie. 'Yuh clean out of options, anyhow.'

No denying that, thought the sheriff, muttering his own curses to the flying sand. There was not even the option in these conditions of chancing his luck on breaking free. First move he made to mount up and Beattie's Colt would be blazing. So maybe sitting it out was the only real choice anybody had. Just sit tight, put your back to the wind and the swirling dirt and wait the hour or so it would take for the calm and silence to creep back like lost souls.

Somebody was already creeping, he thought with a jolt of his numbed senses minutes later at the sound behind the wind of a scuffing of slow, ponderous hoofs, the wincing crease of leather and the soft snorting of a horse.

'Hold it right there, O'Grady,' hissed Beattie, his Colt clearing leather like the lift of a slow black crow. 'This is all mine.'

The scuffing deepened to a gentle thud; more snorting, leather cracking, and then the growing blot of a shape: the mount, the rider bent against the gusts; an easy pace, no threat, no haste.

'Jim?' croaked O'Grady. 'That you there?'

'Quiet!' snapped Beattie, taking a step forward, his free hand gesturing for the back-up of his waiting men.

The mount scuffed to a halt, tossed its mane-tousled head and snorted.

Strange raised his gaze and stared without blinking, without a twitch of nerve across his sand-glazed face.

'Well, I do declare, see what the wind's blown in, boys!' leered Beattie, levelling the Colt. 'Don't that good Lord up there work in the most mysterious ways? Hallelujah, don't He just! And real sight yuh are too, Mr Strange. Been a long ride, eh? Still, we got the weather for it, ain't we? Welcome to Hell!'

The wind chilled the beading of fresh sweat on O'Grady's brow. 'This ain't of my makin', Jim,' he croaked.

Strange nodded as he lowered his head against a snapping gust of wind.

'Where's the stage?' O'Grady hurried on, balancing himself against the blow. 'They all safe? We heard gunfire back there. That your doin'? Yuh cross Lenski?' The wind snarled again. 'There's a train of army wagons trailin' to Fort Benham. Yuh seen 'em? Some roughneck drifters we saw wouldn't be headin' their way by any chance, would they? I figure mebbe, we got our-selves — '

'What the hell's goin' on here?' flared Beattie, swinging his Colt from Strange to O'Grady. 'What yuh discussin' here like a coupla gossipin' whores? This is my show, damnit, *my show*, yuh hear? I don't give a damn about the stage, and what's this about wagons? Yuh reckon for stallin' for time here, O'Grady, yuh got it all wrong. I'm here for one purpose and one purpose only, and I'm lookin' it clean in the face. You, Jim Strange, I'm here for you! The day of reckonin' for my two boys.' He swung round to his men. 'Bring up that body. Let Mr Strange remind himself of what he's done.'

Two men dragged the roped pack mount supporting Virgil's lifeless body to Beattie's side.

'Yuh see this, Mr-goddamn-Strange, yuh see this?' growled Beattie, grabbing a handful of hair and lifting the death-masked, bulging-eyed head of Virgil into Strange's gaze. 'Oh, sure, yuh see it!' he sneered. 'Here to haunt yuh, that's what it is, 'cos yuh know what, this is how you're goin' to be lookin' in just a few short minutes.' He dropped the head, ranged the Colt and took a step forward. 'Should gun yuh down just like yuh did Arran, same as yuh done for Virgil, but that'd be a whole sight too easy, too soon. No, I figure for yuh pleadin' for me to do that, Jim Strange, askin' me to finish yuh.' He holstered the Colt with a thud of barrel and butt to leather. 'So I figure for yuh sufferin' some before this is done,' he yelled across another gusting swirl. 'Step down, mister. Somebody go hold his mount and somebody bring me my bullwhip. Let's see how much blood this two-bit lawman's got in his body!'

The men at Beattie's back began to murmur, shuffle, move like ghost shapes in the storm-grey gloom.

'Ease up there, Moran,' urged O'Grady. 'This ain't the time or the place for it, and it sure as hell ain't the weather! Just leave it, will yuh?'

'*Leave it?*' snarled Beattie, taking a hold of the bullwhip handed to him. 'I ain't leavin' nothin', savin' Strange's blood on this dirt. Don't nobody tell me other. First man to move is dead. Now, step down, Strange. Right now.'

Strange eased himself slowly, deliberately from the saddle, the wind whipping at his clothes, sand swirling, a clutch of dead brush catching at his pants like a skeletal hand.

'Don't do it, Moran,' called O'Grady, struggling against the two men pinning his arms to his side. 'There's army wagons movin' in, right at the back of us. Can't be more than minutes away. And there's them drifters . . . I tell yuh, Moran, there's a heap of trouble brewin'.'

'Shut it!' snapped Beattie, unfurling the whip. 'Army wagons, drifters . . . they can go to hell.' He glared at Strange. 'Yuh got anythin' to say before I get to this?'

Strange lounged his weight to one

hip. 'Just for the record, I shot Lenski back there. I guess yuh figured I would. He weren't a deal of use to nobody. As for Virgil, yep, shot him too. Fair fight, though. Did yuh another favour there.'

'Favour?' sneered Beattie. 'Yuh call that a *favour*? My son, f'Cris'sake?' He spat viciously. 'Dyin's goin' to be a whole sight too good for you, mister.'

'It was Virgil shot Arran that night in Franckton,' said Strange, stiffening to his full height, eyes dark and narrowed against the wind, staring like beams of a freak light. 'Your boys didn't tell yuh that, did they? They wouldn't, o'course. Under threat of their lives and livelihoods from Virgil, weren't they? Wouldn't dare breathe a word as to how it was Arran and Virgil got to rowin' and fightin' over some cheap whore not worth the bother of beddin'. Too drunk to care. Too jealous, one to the other, to see straight, same as they'd always been. Same as yuh raised 'em, Moran; taught 'em to stand tall to a principle: man's got his say and his rights. He should speak and act to 'em — even when it comes to gunnin' his own kin.'

Strange relaxed again. 'Simple as that, Moran. Virgil was just a mite faster, or Arran a shade drunker. Either way, they stood by yuh, pair of 'em. Never let go of the principle. Might almost say it was your finger on the trigger, both times. But don't take my word on it. Ask your boys there. They all saw what happened. Saw it comin'. Go on, ask 'em. See if any one of them's got the guts to save yuh from committing murder here.'

The wind, the howl and whip of it, filled the silence, so that the grind of wheels and slow plod of hoofs approaching from the north seemed like the echoes of ghostly whispers.

20

'Sand — it's like a man, gets everywhere given half a chance!' Mrs Fitzsimmons brushed savagely at the swirl of grit and dirt in her lap, her vast chins rippling deep into the lace ruffles at her neck. 'You would surely know, Miss Devaux?' she added through a gleaming glance.

The actress bit on her lip, stared angrily and took a tighter grip on the levelled Colt.

Hiram Pepperthwaite sweated freely in spite of the blustery wind whipping in a frenzy at the open stage window, and blinked like a short-sighted lizard behind his smudged spectacles. Captain Pendrew, seated next to him, glared defiantly at Francine Devaux between hurried glances at the raging storm.

'No saying, of course, what's happening out there, is there?' said the colonel's wife on the twitch of a half grin. 'Poor Mr Wethers having to control his team in such conditions. Do hope the horses don't spook. Animals can be quite unpredictable at times like this. Mr Daggs and his men would fall into that category, wouldn't they?'

Francine Devaux squirmed and bit on her lip again.

The stage rocked against a vicious blast of wind.

Sand swirled. Horses snorted. Somewhere, as if at a great distance on the back of the wind, Spruce's shout and murmured words for calm, drifted like echoes.

'I suppose those misguided vermin out there will have the good sense to look to their weapons once the storm has passed,' continued Mrs Fitzsimmons, adjusting the set of her hat. 'Sand can be quite a hazard to the functioning of triggers, chambers, barrels and the like. Wouldn't you say so, Captain Pendrew?'

'Oh, quite so, ma'am,' answered the captain. 'Why, I recall — '

'The colonel has always been most particular about that aspect of his training. 'Guns', he would often say, 'are only tools in the hands of men. But pay them scant heed and the price comes high'.' Mrs Fitzsimmons leaned back dramatically. 'Are you paying that Colt its proper regard, Miss Devaux?' she smiled. 'Would be something of a disaster if it failed you for a grain of sand, wouldn't it?'

Pepperthwaite's face bubbled bright, beading sweat. Captain Pendrew squirmed.

'Still,' said the colonel's wife, relaxing, 'perhaps it won't be necessary. Perhaps this storm is something of a saviour for all concerned. I do quite seriously believe in Fate stepping in. Take that incident — '

'Will you just shut your mouth!' snapped the actress, gesturing with the Colt. 'I'm tired of hearing it. Tired of you too, so I suggest — '

'Well, now, Miss Devaux,' tut-tutted Mrs Fitzsimmons, 'that is no frame of mind to be in at a time like this. You really should stay calm and collected. Your compatriot, Mr Daggs, is depending on you. Tempers among thieves are not to be recommended.'

'I said shut your mouth!' clipped Francine Devaux. 'One more peep out of you and I'll . . . '

'But you wouldn't, would you?' grinned the woman. 'I doubt very much if you have the stomach for it. Isn't seduction more your line, my dear? Soft lights, silk sheets, scent and second-rate sophistication . . . Oh, yes, I am sure that is much to be preferred.'

Francine Devaux's patience snapped like a taut cord stretched the half-inch too far. She stiffened, snarled, sat forward, jabbing the Colt ahead of her like a threatening blade.

Pepperthwaite tensed and screwed his eyes against the roar of the shot he was sure was about to explode.

Pendrew hesitated only seconds, time

to take a breath, gather his senses, before bringing his hand down on the Colt and Francine Devaux's wrist like a bolt of lightning out of the storm.

The actress hissed, spat, wrestled against the grip, her eyes flashing, hair tossing wildly about her head.

Mrs Fitzsimmons had already tensed, every muscle in her formidable bulk summoning its strength for the swinging, swiping punch that when it came landed a clenched rock-hard fist square on Francine Devaux's chin.

The round moon-eyes widened for a moment, seemed to flare as if suddenly torched, then closed instantly as the actress slumped back unconscious.

'Perfect,' announced Mrs Fitzsimmons, slapping her hands together. 'Well done, Captain Pendrew. You are to be commended. Yes, indeed! Now, my friends, we have an edge, as they say.'

★ ★ ★

Spruce Wethers spat the sand from his parched gums and listened to the wind howl and scream through his head like a runaway steam train.

'Hell's-devils!' he grated from the depths of a grit-smeared throat as he wrestled helplessly with swinging reins and jangling tack, the prance and stamp of wild-eyed horses. 'Steady there. Whoa now! Easy does it.' His eyes screwed to tight ridges in the sudden swirl of gusting sand. He coughed, spat again, reached for another length of flying leather and peered best he could for a sight of Daggs.

'Yuh lend a hand here, mister?' he shouted over the gusts to where Daggs and his men huddled like a heap of leaning timbers against the face of a rock. 'These horses get to boltin' and we've sure as hell seen the last of 'em!'

A grizzle-faced man stumbled from the group and flung a hand to whatever he could catch.

'Hold on there, fella,' yelled Spruce. 'I gotta look to my passengers.'

'No need for that,' croaked Daggs, shielding his eyes against a thrust of dirt. 'They're safe enough in the stage. Just mind the horses.'

'Still my outfit here,' snapped Spruce. 'Still my responsibility. And I *still* plan on deliverin' 'em to Fort Benham.'

He spun away on the whip of the wind and grabbed for a hold on the stage, inching his way along it towards the door. Quiet enough in there, he thought, growling and spitting more sand from his mouth. Three pairs of eyes concentrated on the Colt in Francine Devaux's hand, he guessed, and not a deal of choice to do other till the storm was blown through. After that . . . Who could say? But, hell, where the devil was Strange? What had happened to Beattie and his rabble, and just how far back were those army wagons?

He had grabbed, groped and heaved to within an arm's length of the stage door, when Captain Pendrew's head appeared in the window space like a dust-coated mask.

'We've got the gun,' he hissed, blinking rapidly against the swirling dirt. 'Miss Devaux is out of it — for now.'

Spruced nodded and clung on. 'I hear yuh,' he croaked. 'But watch her, f'Cris'sake.'

'Any chance you can start moving the stage again?' asked Pendrew, his words spinning on the howling gusts.

You have to be joking, thought Spruce, edging another foot closer. 'No hope,' he groaned. 'Team would never shift.'

'Be a whole lot to our advantage if we could. Are you quite sure, Mr Wethers?'

Hell, of course he was not 'quite sure', not in a situation like this; how could he be when he could see the sense of moving out? Ten, fifteen minutes and he could leave Daggs and his scum floundering in a blind haze of flying sand and brushwood flotsam, maybe with their mounts scattering to follow the stage team. Twenty minutes and he would have the outfit deep enough into the canyon for it to be out of sight. And in a half-hour, the storm could be blown clean through.

'Risky,' he mouthed, tightening his grip. 'Might end up a sight worse off than we are now.'

'But we might not, Mr Wethers,' hissed Pendrew urgently. 'We might not. You'll give it a try?'

Maybe he needed to give everyone a chance; maybe they would sooner be risking breaking their necks than leaving their lives to the whim of Daggs.

And so, come to think of it, would he.

* * *

It took Spruce five struggling, wind-whipped minutes to claw his way round the stage and reach his driving seat on Daggs's blind side. Not, he reckoned, that Daggs was seeing a deal right now save the scarred grey of a rock face.

He had waited then, fingers gripping for a hold against the gusts, eyes no more than slits against the flying dirt. This far, so good, he thought, clearing his mouth of dirt, but the effort needed to reach the seat — not to say staying there! — was going to test his old bones and worn muscles to the full. Not too certain either of them would take the strain. And then there would be the problem . . . 'Hell, just do it!' he had mouthed to himself, tightening his grip for the lift, timing it for that one brief moment in the swirls when the storm seemed to catch its breath.

He heaved, pulled, gasped, groaned and fell across the seat like a tossed sack of oats. But no shouts of warning from Daggs's men, nothing from drizzle-face still struggling with the tangle of tack. Only the wind, the whipping dirt, clouds of swirling sand, the curtain of storm.

This might just work, he thought, fighting to free the tied reins — might, *if* he could stay seated and balanced, *if* the team were not too spooked to race clean out of their skins, *if* he could hold them, and *if* he got real lucky and pounded the whole shuddering outfit clear of rocks, ruts and hidden snags.

More *ifs* there than one man in his right mind should get to pondering!

He waited again, turned his narrowed gaze over what he could see — the blurred shapes of Daggs and his rabble at the rock face, grizzle-face still struggling with tack, the few yards of the trail ahead leading to the mass of a seemingly blank, impenetrable wall, cloud and land, light and dark, dirt and sand merged now into one almighty emptiness — listened for a moment to the next gathering growl of wind at his back, then cracked the reins into life, whooped his call for the team to move, and prayed the shortest prayer of his life: 'God help us!'

21

'I am not for turning back, gentlemen. Not under any circumstances. These wagons are destined for Fort Benham, and that is where they will be delivered.' The wind-licked, fresh face of the young officer bloomed a touch redder under the effort of his barked words as he stood his ground ahead of his men and stared defiantly over the faces of Moran Beattie, Jim Strange and Sheriff O'Grady.

'Admire your pluck, mister,' growled Beattie, flexing the bullwhip loosely at his side, 'but if what these men here are tellin' yuh is fact — and I seen them scum raiders with my own eyes — yuh ain't goin' no place without a sight more guns standin' to yuh. So I'd reckon your happenin' our way is real good fortune, wouldn't yuh say?'

'I grant yuh that, Mr Beattie,' said

the officer, shifting for his balance against a howling gust, 'and if you and your men would care to join me — '

'We got a stage stranded middle of all this,' snapped O'Grady, wiping the dirt from his cheeks. 'Passengers . . . the colonel's wife among them.'

'That is another consideration,' granted the officer, holding tight to his hat.

'You bet it is!' scoffed Beattie. 'Don't come much bigger in your book, mister.'

'We're wastin' time here,' urged O'Grady. 'We should be movin'. So what yuh figure?'

'Trail tight, best speed we can manage 'til the storm's blown out,' said Strange. 'We stay this side of the canyon. Minute we spot the stage, or the raiders, we hang back. No shootin' 'til we got clear targets.'

'Raiders might not be so generous,' sneered Beattie.

The officer nodded and grunted. 'Agreed, and I'm obliged. But might I ask how it is you men are here? Hardly the place to be of choice, surely? Fortunate for me, of course, that I trailed up to you. So are you here, or going some place, on business? Fort Benham perhaps?'

'Yuh could say that,' said O'Grady.

'Unfinished business,' growled Beattie, glancing at Strange.

The officer nodded again. 'Then we'll not delay.' He turned, hovered for a moment against a buffeting, and strode back to his men at the wagons.

'This ain't done, Strange,' croaked Beattie, flicking the whip. 'Don't go thinkin' it is. You and me are still comin' to a reckonin'. Bank on it.'

'Don't fret none, Moran. I'll be waitin'.'

'Darned sight more waitin' on us up there,' groaned O'Grady. 'Spruce Wethers and that stage for one . . . '

The crack and whine of gunfire, panicked snorting of horses and the scrape and whirring of spinning wheels across the howling gusts of wind had drowned the sheriff's words almost before they had left his mouth.

⋆ ⋆ ⋆

Mrs Fitzsimmons' feathered hat finally collapsed to a plucked mass and took flight like a bird through the open stage window. The first jolting thrust of the outfit tumbled Hiram Pepperthwaite to the floor where he scrambled blindly for his spectacles. Captain Pendrew, stiffening himself for the bounce of wheels, pushed Francine Devaux deep into the corner seat, her skirts full blown over flailing legs.

'Go for it, Mr Wethers!' yelled the colonel's wife as her mop of grey hair tumbled from its pins.

'Hold on for yuh lives!' bellowed Pendrew, the Colt firm and steady in his hand, gaze tight on the sprawling actress.

Pepperthwaite moaned miserably at the slewing, bucking tilt of the floor, his head filling with the creaking clatter of timbers and spinning wheels, the wild gunfire, snorting and whinnying of the racing team. Hell had erupted, he thought, burst from the very bowels of Two Knees Canyon to rage at will. He would be dead before sundown, a sprawled body in a no-place, nowhere land's dirt . . .

Spruce Wethers cursed, swallowed on a stomach that had already reached his throat, braced himself against the next shattering jolt, but held tight to the whipping reins as if they were a lifeline.

Daggs and his men had made a big mistake in opening fire as they had; gunshots had only served to spook the horses to a wilder frenzy, their instinctive dread of the storm heightened as if lightning had split the skies. But just where, damn it, were they dragging the stage? Pointless trying to hold to a line; the team would race where the head pair led until they were either exhausted or the stage foundered and splintered to matchwood.

Spruce winced at another crashing

bounce, the whine of shots, pound of hoofs gathering at the back of him. Daggs and the raiders had mounted up. Did they have a choice? Hell, they were watching their major pawn in the heist disappearing into the teeth of a canyon storm.

'Few options now, Captain Pendrew,' called Mrs Fitzsimmons above the creaking din. 'We go with the wind! You agree?'

'As you say, ma'am,' groaned the captain, blinking through a haze of dust and sweat. 'Not from the military manuals, but better than doing nothing.'

'I just hope Mr Wethers manages — '

A button-booted foot crashed across Pepperthwaite's head spinning him into the knees of Pendrew who lurched violently to his left, the Colt waving uselessly at the stage roof for the split-second it took for Francine Devaux to make her move.

She kicked again at Pepperthwaite's head, then at the captain's shins, flung a clenched fist across his temple and spat like a saloon bar veteran into the face of Mrs Fitzsimmons.

'You hell-cat — ' began Pendrew on a groan, only to take another lunging fist across his head followed by a clawing drag of fingernails down his cheek and into his neck.

Pendrew fell back, blood bubbling in streaks across his face; Mrs Fitzsimmons groaned, hissed, reached blindly for the snarling, still spitting actress as she plunged to the coach door, flung it open and threw herself headlong into the snapping wind and swirling dirt.

Spruce caught the blur of the open door and the figure tumbling through it in the corner of his eye. 'Hell!' he groaned, heaving frantically on the reins, cursing the team to a halt — and wasting his effort and his breath as the outfit plunged on into the swirling curtain of wind-driven dirt.

The coach door thudded shut again under the momentum of the sway and bounce. Mrs Fitzsimmons grimaced and swore quietly to herself as she cleared the spittle from her face. Captain Pendrew fingered the blood on his cheek. 'You all right, ma'am?' he croaked. The colonel's wife merely shuddered the bulk of her bosoms. Pepperthwaite rose from the floor like a mound of flotsam beached from a wreck, blinking behind cracked spectacles, the sweat gleaming on his face. The coach slewed wildly to the left, bounced, creaked and cracked. And the wind continued to howl.

'Damn the woman, and good riddance,' groaned Pepperthwaite, hoisting a half of his body to a seat. 'Hope she rots in the dirt!'

'We might all be doing just that,' said Pendrew as another echo of gunfire cracked across the howls. 'If we don't get shot first!'

'Just how the devil . . . ' But Pepperthwaite's voice snapped to the sudden leap of the coach as if it had taken to the air where it seemed to hang for a moment on spinning wheels before crashing back to the ground with a splintering shudder.

Seconds later the outfit, the team, Spruce Wethers and the three bruised, bemused passengers in the coach were still, drained to a silence where there was nothing save the howling wind and the thudding beat of hoofs as Daggs and his men closed like the death riders from Hell.

22

'Spruce has made a run for it,' yelled O'Grady above the whipping wind. 'He ain't never goin' to hold that team in this weather — not even him. Darn fool!'

'Get back to the wagons,' called Strange, reining his mount tight to O'Grady's side. 'And for God's sake, keep Beattie outa my hair!'

'What yuh plannin'?'

'Gettin' to them raiders. They're followin'. Ain't nothin' Spruce can do about them. Rats'll shoot everybody in sight.'

'You among 'em!' growled O'Grady, shortening the rein to the lick of another gust. 'I'm comin' with yuh.'

'No, yuh ain't! You do like I say. Keep Beattie out of it and don't let them army types get to wanderin'. Do what yuh can about lendin' a hand, but do it quiet. Yuh got that? No arguin'.' Strange rounded his mount to the darker depths of the canyon. 'Hand me one of them rifles yuh got there.' He waited for O'Grady to draw the Winchester from its scabbard. 'Thanks. It'll come back empty!'

O'Grady waited, mouthing quietly to himself, until Strange and his mount were no more than a blur in the swirling dirt and grey hanging light before reining sharply to the trundling pay wagons.

He was still cursing when he stared deep into Moran Beattie's eyes. But neither man exchanged a word.

★　★　★

'I shall give myself up. Nothing else for it,' announced Mrs Fitzsimmons, dusting a cloud of dirt from her clothes. 'If the man you sent to Fort Benham has made it, my husband will be here within hours; Daggs can do his negotiating and we shall all be safe. I see no alternative.' She pulled defiantly at her stained, torn gloves. 'There *is* no alternative.'

'Nonsense, ma'am,' protested Pendrew, dabbing at the scratches across his cheeks. 'We cannot be a party to such dealing. The colonel — '

'The colonel can do as he wishes, sir! He is largely responsible for this débâcle. What do you say, Mr Wethers? You agree with me?'

Spruce tightened his grip on the stage door and turned his back to the gusting wind. 'No ma'am, can't say I do,' he croaked, spitting the sand from his mouth. 'We ain't done yet. Stage is a mite trashed, I'll grant yuh, but it'll roll. And the team's quiet enough now. All-out exhausted. Daggs is closing on us, but that ain't to say — '

'What about Miss Devaux?' spluttered Pepperthwaite. 'She's maybe still out there somewhere.'

'Couldn't give a damn,' snapped Spruce. 'Her choice, not ours. No, what we gotta do is hold on awhiles. If the colonel gets here and we can somehow muster the pay wagon men to our side, and mebbe, who knows, get Beattie thinkin' straight for once, why there ain't no sayin' to what might happen.'

'That's the spirit, Mr Wethers,' smiled Pendrew. 'Bit of luck here and we outnumber Daggs three-to-one.'

'Are you suggesting we trust to *luck*, sir?' frowned Mrs Fitzsimmons. 'It's been noticeably absent thus far. And unless I'm much mistaken we shall have Daggs and his men surrounding us again in just a very few minutes. I hardly see any *luck* in that!'

'Well — ' began Pendrew.

'It could be — ' followed Pepperthwaite.

'Make room there, will yuh?' croaked Spruce, swinging the coach door open. 'Storm's easin' some and I reckon I just seen somethin'. Move over, will yuh?'

'What have you seen, Mr Wethers?' hissed the colonel's wife. 'Is Daggs here?'

'Oh, he's here, ma'am,' murmured

Spruce settling himself at her side. 'Two shakes of a leg down the trail, and closin' fast. But I seen somethin' else. Somethin' back of the rocks there.'

'What, in Heaven's name?' groaned Pendrew.

'Let's just say our luck's mebbe for changin',' grinned Spruce.

★ ★ ★

Jim Strange had slid from his mount like some loose, drifting shadow, tethered the mare as best he could in the leaning lee of the rocks and bulge of boulders, dropped to one knee in the cover and licked his lips carefully.

His fingers slid softly over the cool steel of the rifle, one hand resting on the stock as his gaze narrowed across the eerie blur of the silent, stationary wagon, the team snorting quietly, flanks still twitching on the effort of the dash, the steam of sweat curling to oblivion on the snap of wind.

They would rest easy now, he

thought, too exhausted to do more than stand and wait on the storm finally blowing itself out. About the same option for Spruce, his passengers and Captain Pendrew huddled deep in the coach; nothing to be gained by trying to go anywhere — but, like the team, no saying how they might spook at the crack of new gunfire.

His gaze shifted anxiously beyond the stage to the still swirling curtain of dust and dirt. Goldman's raiders and the remnants of Pendrew's troopers they were holding prisoner had halted in whatever cover they could find. They would be unaware of Beattie's boys and torn now between sitting it out to wait on a sight of the pay wagons, the arrival of the colonel from Fort Benham, or making a move to secure the stage.

Strange frowned and grunted to himself. No sight of Francine Devaux — so what had happened to her; she riding with the raiders, sitting tight in the stage with that Colt still levelled?

He took a firmer grip on the rifle and

eased a few yards to his left. Time to take a closer look, see just where the raiders were holed-up. He squirmed on, the wind whipping at his clothes, shuffling the sand to drifting waves at his limbs, lifting it suddenly to grey-mist clouds that danced across his eyes like swarms of midges, then waited, listening. Only the howl of the wind, it seemed, but already lowering to a dull, mournful moan as it played itself out. Somewhere the merest tinkle of tack, soft snort of a mount, scrape of a hoof. One of the raiders' mounts? Had to be.

Strange had almost reached the last of the rock cover when a blurred shape passed like a scud of shadow across his vision. He halted, held his breath, watched. The shape moved closer, paused; a hand came to life at its side, fingers idling on the grip of a knife. Another shuffle, closer still. A one-eyed fellow humming quietly to himself, tapping the blade across his thigh, then lifting to flatten it menacingly in the palm of his hand; shuffling on, still humming.

One more shuffle, the one too far, thought Strange, and that would be too close for the scumbag's own comfort.

Strange rose, dark and silent, his two-handed grip knuckle-white on the barrel of the Winchester, the stock cleaving the air, scything the whip of the wind through a swing as vicious in its intent as the clenched teeth snarl on his face. The man paused in his slow shuffle for just a split-second, long enough for his gaze to lift, change from a narrowed, thoughtful stare into nowhere to a wild-eyed look of astonishment and disbelief, before misting to a pained starburst as the stock struck home, felling him instantly.

Strange stood back, dropped to one knee, swung the rifle back to its levelled probe and peered into the dust-shrouded emptiness.

Still only the tinkling tack at a distance, the soft snorts, pawing of a hoof; nothing of shapes, voices, until . . .

'Blades — I want yuh here. Now, damn yuh!'

Strange frowned, eased his grip. He knew that voice, sure he did — Rogan Daggs, so-called big-time gunslinger operating on the fringes of the gambling set Denver way. So that was who Goldman and Francine Devaux had recruited. A poor choice, he reckoned. Daggs was about as trustworthy as a rattler coiled in a bedroll.

'Blades — yuh hearin' me there?'

And impatient as ever by the sound of it. Last Strange had heard of Daggs was on a Wanted bill for the stage robbery at Fawney Springs two years back. Far as he knew, the sonofabitch was still wanted.

'Do I have to come and drag yuh back here?' cracked the voice again on the rush of the wind.

And why not, grinned Strange? Sadly, Blades would be sleeping it off for some while yet!

An angered hawk, spit, groan, and then the crunch of steps.

Strange eased back to the cover. There would be no second chancing this, he thought, not once Daggs reached the first of the sprawl of rocks, saw the body of his sidekick and either slid back to his men or came on, his Colt set to blaze at the first whisper of a breath.

Another scuff of steps, a pause, maybe to wipe a swirl of sand from his face; a croaked, incoherent curse, more spitting, more steps.

'Yuh seen somethin' out here, damn yuh?' called Daggs again.

And then the blur of the man in Strange's line of vision. No Colt drawn as yet and still some yards short of the sidekick's sprawled body. Only a matter of time . . .

Daggs came slowly to the body, silent, his gaze intent for a moment, peering closer, lifting to take in what he could see around him. Damn all, save sand, dirt, rock, the light that seemed to

251

be shifted on the whims of the wind as it began to break clearer and brighter.

Strange tensed. Take a few more steps, mister, this way, towards me. No looking back, no need to call up your men.

Daggs had darted from sight almost before Strange had taken his next blink, slipped like something of the light itself from where he had been less than a yard short of the body — and seemingly disappeared.

Strange flexed his shoulders on a twist of sweat. No time to wait, he decided. O'Grady might be closing on Daggs's men even now. Beattie would have joined him, along of the young officer. If they got too keen, too soon, it would be as good as putting a lighted taper to tinder.

He had risked another glance, eased the few inches above the highest of the rocks, when he heard the cold, metallic click of a gun hammer slipping into place, the soft titter, the easy spout of spittle to stone.

'Might've known,' drawled Daggs at Strange's back. 'Should've figured for some smart gun messin'. Know yuh, don't I? Jim Strange, one-time big noise in Franckton. Comin' down a notch or two, ain't yuh? Still, yuh done your messin' well enough here, grant yuh that. Yuh lookin' for a cut into this, or somethin'? Can always use another hand to my deck if yuh've a mind — '

But Strange's mind was already concentrated, even as Daggs's voice dripped on the wind, as he spun round, the Winchester levelled in a whooshing swish that brought its barrel clean across Daggs's gun hand, swinging the Colt from his grasp, cutting into his wrist and raising a croaked groan of pain to smother his words.

The rifle blazed high and wide to a whining echo in the momentum. 'Damn!' cursed Strange, falling back to Daggs' instant onslaught of flying arms, fists and legs.

The men locked for a moment, hands slithering, sliding, clutching for a grip on shoulders and neck. Strange heaved, locked a boot between Daggs's legs, twisted to send the pair of them crashing to the dirt, blood spurting from the raider's wrist.

'Sonofabitch!' cursed Strange, as Daggs squirmed like a scorched rattler from beneath him, his fingers clawing for the Colt thrown against a rock face. Daggs groaned, kicked out wildly, raising a cloud of sand in Strange's eyes.

The seconds lost as Strange blinked, spat, choked and cleared the sweat-mist from his vision were enough for Daggs to scramble on all-fours, reach the gun and settle it tight in his grip.

He scrambled upright, his body tensed on a straddled stance, eyes gleaming, a snarl twisted to a grin oozing trickles of saliva. 'Yuh sure as hell relish the messin', don't yuh?' he croaked. 'What's with you, Strange? What yuh — '

But it was the hesitation, the time spent spitting words when a blaze of lead might have settled the issue, that left Strange still breathing as the first of the gunfire among Daggs's waiting men split across the wind as if ripping through taut canvas.

O'Grady had found them, thought Strange, watching the grin on Daggs's face drift to an open mouth, his glance range over the half light, the dirt-streaked curtain.

'More of your messin'?' mouthed Daggs, the glance flicking back to where Strange should have been, except now there was no more than a space and the wind whistling through it. 'Hell's devil!' he grunted and swung round again, this time to the restive snorts, whinnying and prancing of hoofs from the stage team deeper in the canyon. 'Strange!' he bellowed, coming to his full height. 'Strange!'

The gunfire roared and echoed. Horses snorted. The shouts, screams, groans of men crowded the air deadening the storm howl to a whimper. The blurred shapes of riders, hung low to the necks of their mounts, cluttered Daggs's bewildered gaze as Two Knees Canyon erupted, the air thickened with cordite and even the swirling dirt seemed to retreat underground.

'Strange!'

Daggs would not have heard the scuff of steps through the churned rippled sand until the shape was there, grey and shadowy like the breath of some passing ghost. A silent shape, relaxed now and easy, only half-turned to face him, the brim of the hat pulled low against the wind, the eyes watching him as if lit by the lick of high flames behind them.

He would have been aware of the last of his raiders scattering to wherever there was not a gun waiting for them; of the arrival of strange faces, riders not seen before, of the gleam of a Sheriff's badge, of troopers, a young officer, of one man who sat his mount like some vast hunched crow and simply watched.

He would have heard the voices calling from the stage, the shouting, thud of more hoofs, the barked orders halting a tack-jangling troop; the thunderous voice of that lavender-scented, corset-creaking woman 'Gerald! A word. Immediately!' — and then, it seemed, of an uncanny silence, the storm wind dying, the dirt settled and still.

Only then would his stare have gone back to the half-turned shape at the rocks. But now the Colt was heavy in his hand, the sweat thick and hot in his neck, his eyes misting, so that he saw the Winchester rise slowly in the man's grip, level without hurry, blaze without him hearing the roar and lower again without seeming to move.

And then there was nothing at all to see . . .

23

'Yuh said it, Jim Strange. Said it loud and clear. And I heard every goddamn word! So you just step outa this office and go ahead and do it. Why the hell should I care?'

Sheriff O'Grady slumped back on the chair behind his desk and stared hard into the eyes of the man facing him. 'Well, what yuh waitin' for?' he asked, the soft grin playing mischievously at his lips. 'Yuh got a fine day for it, ain't yuh? Sun's up, sky's clear, town's quiet, folk ain't frettin'; even the dogs are dozin'.' His eyes gleamed for a moment. 'And Moran Beattie is waitin' on yuh patient as yuh like. Why, all yuh gotta do is open that door back of yuh, step to the boardwalk, hitch yuh pants, finger them Colts and stride right up to the Sweetcall Bar, push open the batwings — and there yuh are.' He stretched his arms in a wide, generous gesture. 'Simple as that. Doubt if Beattie'll know what hit him!'

Jim Strange stiffened on a sharp intake of breath and tightened the line of his lips. 'Yuh all through with this?' he snapped.

'No, I ain't,' flared O'Grady, coming to his feet, his hands flat on the desk. 'Not by a long shot, I ain't! I ain't for seein' you makin' a whole heap of new trouble for y'self, and I ain't for bein' the one expected to clean it up.'

He straightened, slid his thumbs to his belt and crossed from behind the desk to the dusty, sunlit window, conscious of Strange's gaze following him like a perched buzzard eyeing its prey. 'Been a whole month now, Jim, since Two Canyons,' he went on quietly, scanning the street. 'Whole lot happened since then, lives changed, folk taken to new paths, some lost forever like that actress woman we never did find, not so much as a bone of her — but, hell, we came outa that mess alive, pair of us, and we got plenty to be thankful for in that.'

O'Grady turned, a brighter, piercing gleam in his eyes. 'You especially. Hell, yuh stood here, in this office, m'self along of yuh, Moran Beattie standin' at the far end, and yuh heard same as I did what he said. How'd he put it? Said as he took back everythin' he'd levelled against yuh; said, straight up, as how his boys had told him what really happened to Arran that night and that no blame fell to you. Saw that now — *he said so!* I heard him. And I heard him say too as how Virgil had deserved no better than he got. Fellow stands to another in a drawn fight, and the rules are fair.'

O'Grady swallowed. 'Beattie might be a barrel of trash in many ways, but he knows the rules and he plays to 'em. Expected his own to do the same.' He waited a moment, his gaze steady, unblinking. 'Yuh got an apology from him over Lenski and Joe Reisner, didn't yuh? *An apology*, f'Cris'sake!

From Moran Beattie! Ain't never been known.'

The sheriff walked carefully back to his desk, seated himself, leaned back and folded his arms. 'Then what did he say? Yuh recall, don't yuh? Said he'd personally see to it with them politician friends of his back East that you were reinstated as Sheriff of Franckton and not a mark made to your record.'

O'Grady rocked back in the chair. 'Well, I see yuh wearin' the badge again, and I'm seeing yuh large as life right here in Reuben. And welcome yuh are too, Jim, anytime. Don't have to say it, do I?'

He thudded the chair back to its four legs and slapped his hands palms down on the desk. 'But if you're hidin' behind that badge of law in my town with thoughts of still settlin' some old score with Moran Beattie across there at the Sweetcall, I tell yuh straight yuh got the wrong town, the wrong day, and, sure as hell, the wrong man to be tellin' it to!

'It's over. Done. Finished. No goin'

back. Only place is the future. So what yuh goin' to do, Jim? Yuh goin' to join Beattie for a drink out there, or yuh goin' to kill him? Straight choice to my thinkin'. So what'll it be? Tell me. I'm waitin' . . . '

★ ★ ★

Jim Strange, the no quarter given, none expected, reinstated Sheriff of Franckton, chose the drink and the prospect of the future and was to spend much of his remaining years as a Midwest lawman counting Moran Beattie among those he reckoned he could trust.

Spruce Wethers continued to be the first and most reliable stage driver on the fortnightly Reuben to Fort Benham run the line had ever seen. He finally came to his 'quieter days' managing the swing station at Cooney Forks.

Quieter days came a deal sooner for Colonel Gerald Fitzsimmons. Although commended officially by the military hierarchy back East for his 'speed and efficient response to the attempted robbery of army pay wagons at Two Knees Canyon and the subsequent arrest of the few who could still be rounded up following the attempt', the colonel expressed the view, 'with much regret', that the time had maybe come to take his retirement and leave the chain of command at Fort Benham in younger hands. His decision was accepted and the incident passed into military history.

★　★　★

Some, of course — Sheriff O'Grady, Jim Strange, Spruce Wethers in particular — had other ideas on the force behind that decision, 'namin' no names!' as Spruce had put it.

But it was Hiram Pepperthwaite who was to witness the final act of what is still talked of as the 'black day at Two Knees'.

The town was Nantsville, sixty miles due south of Kansas; a one-street, one-eyed huddle on the stage line to the border in which Pepperthwaite had arrived to join the mourners at the funeral of his long-time friend, John Carter.

That part of his duty done and respects paid, he had eaten frugally at the town's rundown hotel, spent an hour reading the pages of a month-old newspaper, consulted his timepiece frequently to check that the hands were indeed moving towards three-o'clock and the scheduled arrival of the stage northbound when, crossing the street to the line office, he had been joined by a small, neat, fussy fellow clutching a polished leather valise.

'Say, you must be travellin' along of me,' the fellow had smiled. 'That so? Well, sure am pleased to make your acquaintance, mister. Nothin' like havin' somebody to pass the time of day with when you're travellin', is there?'

Falling quickly into step at Pepperthwaite's side, the man had continued: 'But, heck, we sure got one helluva treat for the likes of us fellas travellin' t'day. Yessir! Guess who's ridin' along of us. Yuh can't? I'll tell yuh. None other, mister, than Esther Costelle. In person! Yuh heard of her, o'course, ain't yuh? Esther Costelle — the actress! Eyes like moons . . . '

Pepperthwaite had halted, stared, sweated behind his steel-rimmed spectacles.

'Thought that might shake yuh,' the fussy man had grinned. 'Mention of that name and the blood gets to boilin', eh? Sure does. 'Course, I ain't seen too much of her performin', and they say that ain't her real name — goes sorta incognito, I guess — but old pal of mine out Utah way tells me he once saw her, front row too, playin' Lady Macbeth like he ain't never seen before. Why, he reckons . . . Where yuh goin', mister? Stage leaves in a half-hour.'

Last anyone heard of Hiram J. Pepperthwaite, he was living alone somewhere out Montana. Damn near a hermit, they reckoned, who never went no place.

So they say.

THE END

We do hope that you have enjoyed reading this large print book.

Did you know that all of our titles are available for purchase?

We publish a wide range of high quality large print books including:
Romances, Mysteries, Classics
General Fiction
Non Fiction and Westerns

Special interest titles available in large print are:
The Little Oxford Dictionary
Music Book, Song Book
Hymn Book, Service Book

Also available from us courtesy of Oxford University Press:
Young Readers' Dictionary
(large print edition)
Young Readers' Thesaurus
(large print edition)

For further information or a free brochure, please contact us at:
Ulverscroft Large Print Books Ltd.,
The Green, Bradgate Road, Anstey,
Leicester, LE7 7FU, England.
Tel: (00 44) **0116 236 4325**
Fax: (00 44) **0116 234 0205**

STONE MOUNTAIN

Concho Bradley

The stage robbery had been accomplished by an old woman. Twine Fourch had never heard of a female being a highway robber before. He followed the trail all the way to a dilapidated log cabin up Stone Mountain. What happened after that no one could believe even after townsmen from Jefferson found the old log house and the skeletal dying old woman. But before the mystery could be solved there would be two unnecessary killings, a bizarre suicide and a lynching.

GUNS OF THE GAMBLER

M. Duggan

Destitute gambler Ben Crow arrives in Mallory keen to claim his inheritance, only to discover that rancher Edward Bacon has other ideas. Set up by Miss Dorothy, who had fooled him completely, Ben finds himself dangling on the end of a rope. Saved from death, Ben sets off in pursuit of Miss Dorothy, determined upon retribution. However, his quest for vengeance turns into a rescue mission when she is kidnapped by a crazy man-burning bandit.

SIDEWINDER

John Dyson

All Flynn wants is to be Marshal of Tucson, but he is framed by the territory's richest rancher, Frank Buchanan, and thrown into Yuma prison. Five years later Flynn comes out, intent on clearing his name and burning for vengeance. Fists thud, knives flash and bullets fly as he rides both sides of the law and participates in kidnapping and double-dealing. He is once again arrested for a murder of which he is innocent. Can he escape the noose a second time?

THE BLOODING OF JETHRO

Frank Fields

When Jethro Smith's family is murdered by outlaws, vengeance is the one thing on his mind. He meets the brother of one of the murderers, who attempts to exploit Jethro's grudge in the pursuit of his own vendetta. The local preacher, formerly a sheriff, teaches Jethro how to use a gun. With his new-found skills, Jethro and his somewhat unwelcome friend pit themselves against seemingly impossible odds. Whatever the outcome lead would surely fly.

SEVEN HELLS AND A SIXGUN

Jack Greer

Jim Cayman had been warned about Daphne Rankin, his boss's wife, and her little ways. When Daphne made a play for Jim and he resisted, the result was painful and about what he had feared. But suddenly matters went beyond the expected and he found himself left to die an awful death. Only then did he realise that there was far more than a woman scorned. He vowed that if he could escape from the hell-hole he would surely solve the mystery — and settle some scores.